CW01521528

bad sex
fiction and essays
is good

Other Books by Jane DeLynn

Some Do

In Thrall

Real Estate

Don Juan in the Village

bad sex

fiction and essays

is good

Jane DeLynn

Painted Leaf Press

New York City

This is a work of fiction. The characters, incidents, places, dialogues and speeches are products of the author's imagination and are not to be construed as real. The author's use of names of actual persons living or dead is incidental to the purposes of the plot and is not intended to change the entirely fictional character of the work.

copyright © April 1998 by Jane DeLynn

All rights reserved. No part of this book may be reproduced or transmitted in any form or by any means, electronic or mechanical, including photocopying, recording, or by any information storage and retrieval system, without permission in writing by the publisher.

Published by Painted Leaf Press, 308 W. 40th Street, New York, N.Y. 10018

Manufactured in the United States of America

Cover Design by James Maszle
Text Design by Brian Brunius

Library of Congress Cataloging-in-Publication Data

DeLynn, Jane.
    Bad sex is good / Jane DeLynn.
       p.   cm.
    ISBN 1-891305-00-X
    I. Title.
    PS3554.E4465B33   1998
    813' .54--dc21   97-43660
                                         CIP

For all the girls I used to love—

who inspired these stories & others,

but especially for my friend Cathy

Table of Contents

Author's Note

Although books like this don't usually include sections of an author's previously published novels, I have done so here, because those novels are long out of print and I see no other way anyone could have access to what is in them. If a section is from a novel, I say so at the end of the piece, even if the novel has as yet not been published, as is the case with *Hyacinths* and the novel tentatively entitled *Assumption of the Leash*.

The work itself (mostly fiction, but also an article and essay) was written over the course of more than two decades, and the tone and subject matter vary considerably. Some of what I wrote I would write differently today; some I would not write at all. Certainly my views of many things have changed. But although the temptation to rewrite is considerable, I decided to let the pieces remain as they were written (save for the occasional egregious boo-boo). They're true to their time, and that semi-stranger who wrote them. Who's to say I know more than her anyway?

bad sex
fiction and essays
is good

Strange Attractors

The major sex organ, it is said, is the one between the ears. I prefer to think it is not just the brain itself that is referred to, but the organs of sensation and perception that are lodged in the uppermost part of the body: the eyes, the ear, the nose, the tongue—and others, perhaps, for which there is currently no name.

The events I will be referring to took place long ago, when the cynical idealism of youth had not yet given way to the idealistic cynicism of middle age. I had more energy then, and time, to devote to the amorous arts, and my sexual vanity was naturally not so considerable as it is today. (I use 'vanity' not in the usual pejorative sense of 'vainglorious' or 'excessively proud,' but as regards the very essence of its meaning: 'without real significance or value.') For it was an age when, you see, I still believed in the meaning—both iconographic and 'real'—of those acts of excitement and distress that generally occur between two (but on occasion three or four or even more!) people who find themselves in some way or other sometimes sexually, but perhaps more often economically or socially—'attracted' to each other.

I was involved with a woman with whom I had little in common. Our sole shared interest was the theater, for we had met when she had had the starring role in a play I had written—a rather gloomy affair that, although I still include it in my CV, I would never allow to be shown to an agent. Although her combination of 'vanity' (in the standard sense) and reticence had for some reason driven me wild from the moment I had seen her, and led to tedious and prolonged negotiations with the producer and director over whether or not to 'hire' her—a word I use loosely, for in the downtown theater of those days remuneration tended to be hypothetical rather than actual—she was not particularly effective in the role. But who would have been, given the dialogue she was forced to recite? Have I omitted to mention she was quite beautiful?—delicate, with lovely dark coloring on which a kind of permanent natural blush resided, albeit her brown eyes emanated what to me seemed a rather irritating cow-like placidity.

We were poor then, she even more so than me, and could rarely afford to go to restaurants. Our evenings tended to consist of her cooking me some sort of vegetarian concoction, the consumption of an illegal substance or two (accompanied by, on occasion, a legal one such as beer or wine), and the listening to records, sometimes preceded or succeeded by our attendance at a movie or performance at the kind of inexpensive theater in which my own had first seen the light of—well, night. On occasion we passed the evening in my apartment, but unbeknownst to her my (male, gay) roommate found her company monotonous in the extreme, so generally I created an excuse to stay in hers.

Having little in common (besides which she was not talkative), our conversation consisted almost exclusively of pleasantries concerning plays we had seen or were thinking of see-ing, and instruction as to how to properly prepare vegetables. For variety we discussed yoga, which she practiced and I pre-tended I wanted to. The rest of the time, we were either silent, or I, the Writer, held forth, sometimes on my current *kvetches* and sometimes on my childhood. (Sometimes, these were the same.) In spite/because of the tedium of conversa-tion and the ritual predictability of our encounters, I loved her madly. Because she meditated, because she practiced yoga, because she abjured the incensing effects of meat, I could never decide whether her conversational reticence was due to some flaw such as shyness or lack of intelligence (or, at least quick-wittedness), or was, conversely, evidence of some profounder wisdom having to do with the pointlessness of speech and the 'vanity' (in *my* sense) of all endeavor. When on occasion I made inquiries into the causality of her sereni-ty, she would inevitably remain motionless for several min-utes, then a peculiar smile would pass across her face, her nostrils would dilate, and she'd give a beatific shrug. It was a response identical in spirit (and almost so in appearance) to her inevitable response of 'nothing' when I would interrogate her as to what she was thinking.

In those days I thought I knew everything—not just about the world but about myself and other people, including thoughts and feelings that supposedly resided in the uncon-scious—so I rarely took people at their word, but would probe beneath surface speech and actions for the hidden meaning I was sure I could somehow divine. My next-to-most recent therapist ascribed such attitudes to 'grandiosity,' but I think it had more to do with boredom. When I did not find the world (rather, that particular part of it on which I was cur-rently bestowing my attention) worthy of my interest, I would simply invent the sub-text to make it so. Indeed, is not Love the invention of a sub-text so coherent, persuasive, and enthralling that, on occasion, the narrative it creates so over-powers the apparent commonsensical one that no amount of contrary or even contradictory 'real world evidence' can have the slightest a/effect on its shape? Thus, when Mirabelle (for such was her name) replied "I don't know" to a question of whether Presidents Kennedy, Johnson, or Nixon would be judged by God (should S/He exist) most culpable in relation to the Vietnamese (against whom our war had only recently *officially* ended), I did not even consider accepting this reply at face value—as a simple acknowledgment of insufficient confidence in her knowledge and/or judgment—but fabricated in my mind an unspoken monologue which provided a resonant and intellectually worthy explanation for her only *apparently* vapid and non-committal utterance, as well as giving a sympathetic and morally admirable reason for not disclosing such explanation to me: the well-intentioned (but—on some deep level—profoundly naive) questioner.

It is hard to recreate such internal monologues, but to the best of my recollection this one ran something as following:

"Johnson and Nixon are mass murderers. . .everybody knows that.

"She threw Kennedy in there to irritate me—knowing I and everybody else like him—we have discussed this before and what would be the point of hashing it through again?

"In such instances of villainy, which of the two is worse hardly matters-nor do I believe she thinks it matters. She just wants to argue with me no matter whom I pick.

"Because I see no point in arguing, I'll reply 'I don't know,' rather than telling her there is no point to her question, for although she surely knows it herself, my articulation of it will hurt her, she is so sensitive. After all, is it not better for me to look 'stupid' than her, since my ego is so much less invested in intelligence than hers?"

On the night in question we had gone to an inexpensive play in an East Village theater in which the actors were paid by the sharing of the gate receipts—an amount that one could not even count on to cover the requisite post-performance repast. It was a play in which, as was common in those days (as in ours- not to mention Shakespeare's) male actors assumed female roles. At the time I was more excited by the nuances of gender confusion than feminism, so the logical corollary—why were women not assuming the roles of men?—did not occur to me. I had, in short, enjoyed the play, and so, to all appearance, had Mirabelle.

We bought some beer and climbed the steps to her sixth floor apartment. Her building was in the heart of the old Greenwich Village, and, by dint of the fortuitous placement of nearby buildings, commanded a clear view of surrounding rooftops and a sliver of the Hudson. This night, with perhaps a quarter moon, you could discern, if you squinted your eyes, whitecaps on the river; several blocks south a crowded and brightly illuminated rooftop gave strong indication that a movie was being shot. Inexplicably (and therefore tantalizingly), the set consisted of a little wooden house, several café tables and an old-fashioned telephone booth.

We sat in our usual silence while watching the proceedings, then of a sudden the bright lights dimmed, taking with them, so I felt, a bit of the magic of the evening. Mirabelle must have experienced something similar, for almost immediately she got up and asked if I would like her to put on some music, which until that moment we had managed to do without.

"Please."

She squatted on her knees, pawing through the records till she found some Keith Jarrett, who served the function then that New Age music would later in the decade. "Would you like another beer?"

"Sure," I said. But she did not take another for herself, so I sipped mine very slowly. I would have pounded the top back on the bottle would that not have looked like I could not make a decision for myself.

I talked for awhile about the play itself, and then the acting (which—having been trained in some watered-down version of The Method—she denounced for focusing too much on such 'surfacey externals' as vocal intonation and bodily gesture), then she went into the bedroom and came out with a little wooden box which contained illegal but nonetheless relatively inexpensive products of the hemp plant. Sitting on the floor beside the coffee table, she spread out a piece of paper and began sifting out the dried-up flowers from the seeds and twigs. She was frugal and always performed this part of the operation slowly and delicately, whereas I, less conscientious and meticulous, would invariably lose patience, and end up with little sticks poking their way through the papers of my joints.

When she was done, she placed a single sheet of the white rolling paper on the table, then carefully sprinkled a thin and even line of the herb across it. After smoothing out this row, and winding the paper in a tight little cylinder so that it would burn slowly and evenly, having twisted one end closed and the other somewhat less so (so as to allow sufficient passage of air to maintain combustion), she placed just enough saliva on the yellow glue strip to ensure the seal would hold, while nonetheless allowing the paper to remain sufficiently and miraculously dry. Mine inevitably dissolved into a soggy mess that was not just esthetically unpleasant but created almost insurmountable difficulties in both lighting and sustained smoking.

Although with insufficient patience to roll an adequate joint myself, I somehow always possessed more than enough to cheerfully witness these slow and somewhat self-absorbed preparations.

"Here," she said, extending the exquisitely-made object to me. She always offered me the first hit, and for some reason this ceremonial politeness never failed to enchant me. Although smoking marijuana in large groups often made me nervous, and could unnerve me even in her presence, I always forced myself to accompany her in her ingestion of the various stimulants and relaxants and hallucinogens, for fear that we would no longer be able to converse at all if our bodies were not being affected by the same constituency of chemicals.

"Thanks."

She struck a match and leaned over. The light isolated and made even more striking the angles of her cheekbones. Then the end of the cigarette began to glow red, and I tried to stifle a cough.

After several hits, I handed the joint to her. She inhaled, then leaned her head against the base of the couch and shut her eyes. The cigarette dangled from her fingers, but due to the skill with which she had rolled it, it neither died out nor consumed itself. It made me nervous hanging there, but I dared not remove it from her fingers lest she think I was trying to censor her activities.

The slow dilation of her nostrils provided the only indication she was alive. As usual, it was impossible to tell if she were asleep or merely ruminating. The question of which, irrelevant though it might prove to the objective correlatives, was of immense import to me, providing a framework, as it were, for my creation of the sub-text. That is, as long as I continued to believe she was in a meditative state my brain would continue its invention of her internal monologue, but such narration would immediately cease were I to determine she was sleeping, This, in turn, would cause me to become both bored and irritated, both because I would have nothing to fill my mind and because of the consequent likelihood that our sexual activities would be curtailed or even eliminated.

Perhaps this is the place to interject that, not considering herself truly one of the tribe that prefers women (and, indeed, being embarrassed to the point of concealment by such relations with me), my endeavors towards her in that direction were generally far more abbreviated and constrained than they would have been with someone who did not dispute the propriety of such actions. This should not imply, however, that I did not enjoy sex with her. On the contrary, I enjoyed it all the more due to its unpredictable character.

Even the lack of passion (indeed, *distaste)* with which she on occasion stroked my body had ceased to disturb me, for this very apathy—by eliminating the self-consciousness I tended to feel concerning the intensity of my reactions—tended to relax and soothe me, thereby making it easier to achieve the magnitude of response that so often eluded me in the presence of those possessing greater expertise and fervor.

To put it another way, the reflexive perversity of my reactions—my unconscious inability to acquiesce to another's desire to arouse me—lost its compulsive quality in the presence of her indifference, and for perhaps the first time in my life I was able to sexually respond to someone in a relatively straightforward, unstylized fashion.

So when I asked her what she was thinking, it was not because I had reason to expect any answer other than the usual, but because I was anxious to determine the degree of her alertness. To be sure, I was aware of the tenuousness of the approach; sometimes even when she was awake she would choose not to reply to what (after all) seemed to her my redundant inquiries.

"I was trying to remember the words of this song."

"What song?"

"The one I'm supposed to perform at the audition tomorrow."

"I didn't know you had an audition." This news upset me, for she was particularly anxious about her sleep before such appearances. "Would you play it for me?"

"You'd like to hear it?" she asked, with surprise, as if anything that concerned her had ever not interested me.

"Of course."

She pushed herself to her feet and walked over to the spinet. On it were piled songbooks and on top of these sheet music, which in the dark (the room was illuminated only by two candles) she was compelled to flip through slowly.

As I studied her profile my heart caught with her beauty, and it seemed that, despite the remarks of my roommate, nothing else would ever matter. She sang in a mezzo-soprano with vibrato and often came in a bit late on her notes—for which 'cheapness' of effects my roommate had nothing but the most disparaging comments, even as he (somewhat paradoxically, I felt) refused to concede even the intentionality of such adornments.

After several songs she yawned. Although I enjoyed her singing, I was not distressed at this allusion to slumber. After she had emerged from the bathroom, I quickly brushed my teeth and washed my face, then stripped off my clothes and hopped into bed. She, as usual, remained at her little dressing table, performing the various rituals relating to the removal of makeup and the subsequent application of various night-time conditioning and replenishing lotions. My enjoyment of this—like the rolling of the cigarettes and the discussions about vegetables—never palled. Indeed, though surely part of my interest was due to anticipation of the further possibilities of the evening, I have always enjoyed observing the ablutions and repairments of women—both ones I was involved with and others whom I saw in public toilets during intermissions of sundry artistic events—perhaps (as my previous therapist but two suggested), either because I used to observe my mother doing so, or because I did *not*.

'Love': what is it about? Is it an affliction of the flesh or the soul, or a confluence of the two? Is it a blessing or a curse, or both together? Is it the very personification of the human tendency to waste time—or, conversely, the only activity worth pursuing? How often did I ponder such notions as I watched her, how rarely could I decide the proper answer! Bored as I often was in her presence, how much more so was I in her absence! Perhaps, as my roommate complained, there was no 'there there.' Perchance, as my roommate contended, the true locus of her existence was only in my imagination. Quite possibly, as my roommate proclaimed, I had invented her not so much to ward off the Void (as I grandiosely told myself), but because I had lost confidence in my ability to attract someone with greater internal resources.

Even were this all true, I did not care. Her quietness, her coldness, her lack of enthusiasm, served as proxies for my own deficiencies in such arenas, and enabled me, conversely, to feel optimistic, enthused, alive.

When she had finished with the dressing table she turned out the light and delicately climbed into bed, where she lay with her back towards me as near the edge as possible. I was used to this and did not mind, though initially it had bothered me. But I had overcome my reluctance at *her* reluctance when I discovered that it could usually be overcome by a show of interest and persistence on my part. "Come here," I said, after I had sidled over to her and placed my hand on her side.

She turned towards me with that weird shrug and a smile. In the dark we stared at each other. I told myself these were the eyes of a tiger, not a cow. I pulled her to me and, very slowly, as if she were a most delicate doll, as if nothing could be more gross than sticking a tongue in another person's mouth, rested my lips lightly on hers.

A long while later, for I broached each new position as delicately as a spy, as surreptitiously as if I were a teenage boy in a movie theater pretending to watch the film even as he fumbles to unhook his date's bra with a single hand, I found myself lying, my head a little raised, near the foot of the bed, with Mirabelle's legs spread in a curling V or U around my neck, her eyes closed and the emblem of a smile (rather than a smile itself) across her lips. She was breathing shallowly but rapidly as I moved my tongue back and forth, then in a counterclockwise circle, initially at low speed and intensity, with an intermittent and casual flick, like the languid exploration of a sleepy snake. And occasionally, for demi-seconds, I did fall asleep, waking with a guilty start which—had our positions been reversed—I would have instantly recognized by the increase in pressure and speed with which that newly-awoken tongue attacked my body, but which change of motion she never seemed to notice. As the minutes transpired I would gradually increase either the speed or the intensity of these motions of my tongue—not so slowly that the conception of progression would utterly disappear from her consciousness, yet slowly enough that the narratives of titillation and frustration, of resistance and submission, could not fail to be—at least in some subliminal fashion—present in her mind. Then on occasion, for brief milliseconds of time, at (and this is most important!) *randomly*-placed intervals—I would cease action altogether, lest the pattern of titillation itself become predictable and, hence, *untitillating*.

In short, there was a conscious structure to my labors, and I worked as hard and thoughtfully at my calling as I did on my scripts, to ensure that the climax would be as intense and thrilling, as unexpected and yet (in retrospect) as dramatically necessary as any play's. My basic strategy, you might say (though of course this was an improvisational art, subject to vicissitudes of mood, moon phase, amount and quality of recent encounters, and the degree of artificial stimulants and relaxants in both our bodies) was to insinuate the notion of 'timelessness' by a slow and consistent pace, for the purpose of creating in Mirabelle's mind a belief that whatever was happening would (in some sense) continue 'forever' (i.e. as long as was necessary), at which point, having alleviated temporal anxiety as to untimely cessation—for surely nothing upsets the delicate balance of orgasm so much as the concept of being rushed (except when, on occasion, it functions in the very opposite fashion!)—I would commence the introduction, by the aforementioned increases in speed or pressure, of the concepts of teleology and finality—hence death—and it was this dialectic of time vs. eternity, of excitement vs. stasis, of epiphanic enlightenment versus innate knowing, that was responsible (I believe) for the extraordinary intensity of the reaction not just of Mirabelle, but (there is no point in being unduly modest!) of virtually everyone who has come in intimate contact with my tongue.

It is unnecessary, of course, to go into detail concerning the standard 'objective correlatives'—heavy breathing, redness of facial skin, 'involuntary' movements and sounds, outpourings of sweat, convulsive graspings of my head and back which are the inevitable (and, when you think of it, rather frightening and repellent) accompaniments to the gaining of such knowledge, and perhaps I should add that I was not wholly averse to the usage of such 'surfacey' externals as melodramatically bucking my body or mimicking my partner's breathing patterns, not unlike the acting style of the theatrical group we had seen earlier in the evening. This served the dual purpose of convincing Mirabelle that we were undergoing analogous experiences (thereby contributing to the— perhaps subliminal—narrative of 'unity') and also, by means of this mimicry, to at least partially *achieve* this unity—on the level of heartbeat and breath, at least, if not of one's innermost *soul*. To be a good lover, I have often said, is to use your ears correctly!

But sometimes, though I did my best to imitate a partner, she would not issue her clues correctly, would insist on breathing faster than her internal state would really justify (possibly in the attempt to create some narrative of her own such as 'call girl' or 'class slut'), and I would have to slow down and re-start, as it were, the entire scenario. Not that one can precisely re-start it—no more than one can duplicate on one night the rhythms and gestures of another—but by changing my pace and activities I would implant, let us say, the notion of 'intermission' in my partner, so that the lack of early fulfillment could be interpreted not as 'failure' (on *either* of our parts), but rather as something inherent to the structure of this particular interaction, something planned, as it were, rather than accidental. And the creation of a belief in the 'purposefulness' of the interaction would resonate with the earlier notion of 'timelessness' so as to transform the self-conscious anxiety-producing question of *whether* one would reach epiphanic fulfillment into the more benign (and curiosity-inducing) one of *in which particular manner* on this particular night would this particular dramatic crisis be resolved.

To put it another way, you might say that I had switched the genre from mystery to that of suspense. And with the return of this rather detached curiosity, there would be room for Eros to creep back in. The particular method of the *intermezzo* might include such *divertimenti* as the licking of the back of the knee, or the massaging of a gum with my tongue, or pulling of hairs from the pubic area in my teeth—anything that would allow us to re-order our breathing and re-group our resources before recommencing the tedious work. For tedious work it sometimes is when (let's not beat about the bush!), exhausted and (therefore) lacking in imaginative resources, one must animate what may momentarily seem like a piece of wiry brillo with the luster and passion of a human being and all its wishes, thoughts, fears, and desires . . .when, to be honest, what may be filling the soul is disgust and revulsion.

I use the words 'disgust' and 'revulsion,' but these are of course secondary emotions laid, as it were, over the more humanist ones of desire and triumph with which the sex act is hopefully accompanied. I am a 'sensualist,' yes, but how much is ordinarily left out of our concept of this word—for is not every lowering of face onto an unknown and untested torso as much a leap of faith into the dark as that of a body into a lake at night, with its possibilities of foul smells, hidden protuberances, and unexpected denizens, not to mention incompatibility of pheromones or rhythms, phobias and fetishes, from all of which there is no turning back—at least if one has been brought up in such a way as to possess the standard quota of good manners?

Possessing such—for better or worse—I invariably felt honor-bound to persist in my task until satisfied hands clutched my hair to the breasts (my head following), the digits gently touching my face and arms and back until moans soften and the tortured breaths of satisfaction become half-snores, or—on the rare occasion—in despair push my fingers from the hopeless task. I believe in such sad moments it is I rather than my partner who experiences the greater distress, for the disheartening sense of failure and guilt, combined with empathy for the unsatisfied and disgruntled state, so evokes in me the utter pointlessness of human endeavor, the utter frailty of human connection and the impossibility of Love, that I become peculiarly undone, and, smitten by the utter vanity of existence, lie almost Lifeless until, miraculously, some such external intrusion as the telephone or the emergence from cloud cover of the sun occurs to make the quiescent reptile active once again. . .pointless, pointless, pointless!

To return to Mirabelle. This particular night, I vowed, would be special. This particular night we would attain heights of bliss as yet unequaled in our (well, really *my)* exertions. This particular night she would be driven to such extremes that those fearsome words—'I love you'—would emerge, undesired but unsuppressible, from her lips. And with the utterance of these magic totems, our relationship would be transformed—the sub-text articulated, the narrative conceded—and she would clasp my arm, chattering gaily, oblivious to all onlookers, as we sauntered carefree down the street. And courtesy of this unharnessed wit, courtesy of the freedom with which she could share all her little secrets with me, her love in turn would flourish, and multiply. . .etcetera.

With such hopes I commenced my efforts, with such hopes I found her legs forming a V or U around my neck, breathing shallowly but rapidly as I moved my tongue back and forth, then in a counterclockwise circle, faster and faster, with occasional demi-seconds of cessation to mix hope with fear, to create a correlative in her mind for the *frissons* of her body, to show her there was nothing—no thought, no movement, no emotion—that I could not affect as I chose. And she came along with me, she was my slave as much as (in another sense) I was hers; I was a musician on her body, the slightest twitch of my fingers or tongue evidenced their immediate effects on her vocal register, her muscle tremors, the emanation of her bodily fluids. And just when she had thought she had reached the apogee, when the waters of her river were about to run into the sea, when the mystery was about to be revealed, the culprit unmasked, I began, ever-so-slightly, to slow down. And though you may think this a crass attempt to conclusively demonstrate to her once and for all the utter dependence of her every flush, her every drop of sweat upon my whims, the truth of it was another matter entirely: we had reached a place where we had never been.

I have mentioned the concept of 'timelessness' before, I believe, but then it was as one-half of the dialectic—one element in the great Western dualities of Life vs. Death, Action vs. Passivity, Diversity vs. Unity, etc. But as our heartbeats slowed in unison, as our breaths began to flatten and smooth, we approached, in the evenness of inhalation and exhalation, via the glacial pace of meditation, that place where not just Time but its opposite (and the duality this represented—'Time vs. Timelessness') disappeared, where the Many did not just become One but where Distinction itself vanished. In short, we had reached a place beyond words, beyond thought, a site where desire and fear, past and future, had no meaning, a locus necessarily devoid of artificial tensions and such cheap dramatic compulsions as climaxes and denouements, a zone without boundary or dimension in which we rode forever at the speed of light on a beam of particles or waves—take your pick!—towards an ageless, soundless, eternal present.

I had never been so *there* with anyone. I licked, not her skin, but the hairs of her skin. I blew on them like the wind moving across grass, and my hairs rose and fell with hers because the wind struck me too, and when I inhaled so did she, Siamese linked at the lungs. . .No, we were closer than that, not just twins but mirror images, identical beings occupying the same place at the same time, unperceived as conterminous due only to the epistemological limitations of a three-dimensional universe. And because I *was* her, I breathed her slow, calm, constant, evenly-spaced breaths, and I knew, had I been in the realm of the dialectic, the dramatic unities would have been revealed as they never had before.

If it was true for me, by definition it was true for her.

A deep peace ran through me/us, and I felt I/we knew everything. I/we lay there immobile for a few minutes, basking; then I realized my arm, where my head was propped, was aching badly.

I needed to move it. But if I moved it, would I not recall her to the world of 'I' and 'you,' of passion and pain, of things that gush and throats that utter superficial (albeit pleasurable) cries of joys?

It would. Because I loved her, because we lie to those we love, because we lie to ourselves to preserve our love, I tried to distract her/me by altering the movements of my tongue. But this was merely a mechanical diversion. I could not stop thinking of my arm and how, if I did not change position soon, circulation would stop completely and I would develop gangrene.

An honest person—a person who would have been willing to admit the evanescence of all that was and is and is to be would have simply rearranged her limbs. But I continued the charade of Oneness and Unity as by the tiniest of (hopefully indiscernible) increments I ever so slowly and uncomfortably maneuvered myself off one arm and onto the other.

These exertions fatigued me, and I began to breathe more quickly. To my surprise she did not match my increased pace, but maintained the slow and constant rhythm of her in- and exhalations, even when (so as to distract her from these breathing changes) I further varied the speed and pressure of my tongue.

Her continued indifference to these fluctuations, demonstrating as it did how thoroughly estranged we had become, so upset me that I knew my only hope of vanquishing my sorrow was by sharing it with her. Thus, in search of the comfort of speech, her breath on my neck, the dab of her tongue against the comer of my lip, I began to inch my way up her body.

But even in the face of this desperate journey she managed to maintain composure. When I lay my head next to hers, when I flicked the tip of her nipple with my reptilian tongue, her steady breathing did not alter in the slightest, save for the slight increase in amplitude of a certain sound, which readily could have been explained by my closer proximity to its source. This noise, which accompanied each inhalation and exhalation, I initially could not identify, familiar though it was, but as I drew ever nearer her lips it became ever more distinct and, somehow, disturbing, reminding me of. . .something. . .on the tip of my tongue. . . .

A snore! She was sleeping! Had been sleeping, perhaps, throughout our entire surf ride on the perfect wave.

●

The defining moments in a person's life are few. Until that moment I had somehow—despite a vast preponderance of evidence to the contrary—managed to preserve the conviction that, given world enough and time (i.e. sufficient energy on my part and the merest tendency towards reciprocity on someone else's) there was no one in the universe whose will could prove resistant to my desires. I had felt that, in some fashion, I knew *everything*, that mere closing of lips and the shutting of eyes were but insufficient barriers to my gnostic infiltrations, that when I lay face to torso with another, the secrets of the Universe would be revealed. If not all-powerful, I was surely omniscient, and what was the sub-text, the narrative I was continually inventing, but the on-going Bible of my world?

Mirabelle's snore, with its irrefutable demonstration of the vanity of my beliefs, the narcissism of my imaginings, the absurdity of my longings, was a concrete refutation of all I had held dear. No Loss of Dialectic, no Oneness, no Conquering of Time; we were neither musician nor slave, but a foolish writer and a tired actress. All we were sharing- perhaps all we had ever shared—was a bed!

And as the force of these revelations sunk into my exhausted brain (for such inventions are the hardest of work!) my Love began to die, so that by the next morning when Mirabelle poured my tea I was as irritable and bored as even my roommate could have desired me to be, and I rushed home to tell him how right he had been to advise me not to waste so much time and energy on one who was so clearly not worthy of my passion.

The Duchess of L.A.

(for Sheree Rose & Bob Flanagan)

My friend Linda used to be an ordinary housewife married to a professor in Westwood, but she had artistic aspirations, and when she and her husband split up she began to hang around with a hip L.A. crowd, people who went to poetry readings, art openings, clubs. She met a poet named Jack who moved in with her and her cats and her two kids.

Jack was nice and a good poet, but sexually he had his quirks. He had been immobilized in a full body cast for six months because of a car accident in his childhood, and the memory of that bondage held him in all. He liked—"needed" is perhaps a better word—to be tied up, spanked, suspended, insulted. Although Linda had begun to make assemblages, she was still pretty much the same nice Jewish housewife she had always been, and she tried to oblige him. Paddles, collars, handcuffs and restraints of various kinds, even a cage for Jack to sleep in, soon made their appearance in the Westwood house. Some of it she kept locked up in a little room where Jack had his desk, but the cage was too large to hide from her children. Her daughter began to spend nights at her father's house; her son quit the high school soccer team and began to indulge in the standard drugs. For brief moments Linda would be very upset about this, then she would dismiss it as one of those things you grow out of in time. One time the fetish closet was broken into, and after that pee began to appear in the morning all over the son's bathroom, which was also the guest bathroom. Her son said it was because if he turned on the light to pee he couldn't get back to sleep: Jack told her it was because of the fetish objects. I kept wondering when Linda would cut it out and find a nice lawyer to marry and take care of the mortgage payments, but one year passed, then another, and Jack was still there.

It is impossible to know human beings. You think you know them and most of the time you do, but then they will do something to surprise you and you can't fit this in with anything else you know about them, and the fact that you have been able to predict with near certainty their actions in the past only adds to this puzzlement. But I still felt like I really knew Linda, that she was only pretending to be this other person and any day would revert back to the one I knew. I was supposed to be the hip person in our relationship, and this change irritated me. Thus, although when I was with her I pretended to admire her new life, I didn't. I had enough friends who wrote, painted, danced, sung; I had been glad to have a friend who was basically just a nice Jewish girl. She now said things like she couldn't feel complete unless she could build objects that expressed the things that had been hidden inside her for years. I suppose everyone has stuff hidden inside them, but the world would be even more cluttered if everyone felt like they had to convert it into bits of metal, wood, and plastic. Nonetheless, I was in the habit of being her friend, and I saw her and Jack whenever they came to New York.

One time I was in L.A., and I stayed for a few days in her house. The son was still peeing all over the bathroom; Linda warned me to be sure to wipe off the toilet seat before sitting on it. Or maybe I should just squat over it, the way you did in Africa or Asia. At night we went to punk clubs where people looked like people had in New York a year or two before—but more so.

"What happened to your furniture?" I asked. We were sitting on cushions in her livingroom, just as if it were 1968.

"It's kind of a long story. . ." said Linda. She looked at Jack.

"Just tell her the truth," said Jack. "It was our night for the club, and things got a little out of hand."

"What club?"

"Oh, just a club that meets sometimes at our house."

"What kind of club destroys the furniture?"

It turned out to be a kind of liberation organization to protect the rights of people to beat, bind, give enemas to, and urinate on each other, as well as perform other similar such acts. Although the focus of the meeting was usually on theory rather than *praxis*, sometimes things got out of hand. Linda was the chairwoman.

"You're kidding!" To my knowledge, Linda had never run anything bigger than a yard sale.

"Jewish women," said Jack. "'they're used to ordering people around."

"Yeah. Everybody wants to be a slave but me." She sighed.

During my stay Linda and Jack had a lot of squabbles. Most of these seemed to revolve around Jack wanting Linda to order him to do things, and Linda refusing to do this. "You're crazy," I told her. "Why don't you make him go shopping and clean up the house? Do the laundry. Wipe up the pee in the bathroom. Give you a massage. Or won't he do stuff like that?"

"He'll do anything I tell him," she assured me smugly. "We have a three-month contract."

"What does that mean?"

"He has to do whatever I want for three months, and if he doesn't I have the right to punish him."

"If I were you I'd take advantage of it. You're always telling me how you can't stand housework."

"I know. But it's not that simple."

"So you lock him up in the dog cage at night to make him happy. So what?"

"I can't explain it," she said. "It's very complicated. You really should read this thing I wrote." She went to her desk and pulled out some xeroxed sheets that were stapled together. So Linda had become a philosopher. That night we went over to the house of a woman who was Linda's main slave. She was skinny and pale, as if she hadn't been in the sun in years, and it was obvious Jack was jealous of her. After dinner Judy cleared up and then Linda told her to go into the bedroom and get things ready.

"Can I join you?" asked Jack

"No. But if you want, you can kneel outside the door on your knees and listen to us."

"On my hands and knees or just my knees?"

"On your hands and knees. Don't move. Be sure to tell me if he moves," she said to me. "He'll be punished very severely if he does."

"How?" I asked.

"I'll probably tie him up outside the house all night with a gag in his mouth. It's supposed to rain and he'll catch a cold. Jack hates colds."

"Nobody likes colds," said Jack.

Linda got up to leave the room, then stopped. "If you'd like, you could come inside and watch us," she told me. "It would give you a better sense of what I'm into."

"Judy wouldn't mind?"

Linda gave me a somewhat patronizing smile. "It doesn't matter. After all, she's my slave."

I wasn't really interested in what they were doing, but I felt Linda would be insulted if I told her that, so after a few moments of watching Jack kneel like a dog, I followed her into the bedroom.

Judy was dressed only in her underpants. A number of objects, some of which I had never seen before, were lying on the bed: a whip, hand restraints, a paddle, several metal devices that looked like those things we held the remnants of joints with in the late sixties, short chains with pieces of lead on the ends. Linda told Judy she was going to perform something called "breastwork" on her. She took the things that looked like roach clips and put one on each breast. "Ow," said Judy. Linda pulled on these a bit and asked Judy how she liked it. "It hurts," said Judy. Linda nodded as and with much seriousness told her that was good. Then she took several of the lead pieces and attached the chains to the roach clips. "Ow," Judy said again. Then Linda told Judy to take off her pants. Judy stepped out of the pants and laid herself across Linda's lap. Linda picked up the paddle and began to spank her. But for some reason she wasn't pleased with this and told Judy to get the hairbrush that was lying on the bureau. Linda explained to me how you couldn't use your hand to spank someone because it hurt too much—not the person you're spanking but your hand. The spanking was done in a slow and rather desultory fashion, as if Linda were performing a somewhat tedious but necessary task. Occasionally I peeked out the door at Jack. As commanded, he was kneeling like a dog on all fours. It was hard to sense the connection between these acts and sex, though I don't know exactly what else you could call it.

When the spanking was done, Linda told Judy to put on a pair of latex panties. They were a hideous thick green rubber. Linda told me the point of them was to keep Judy's ass hot, in order to prolong the pain and memory of the spanking after Linda was gone. Then she asked Judy to please make some coffee for herself and me.

"What would you like in it?" Judy asked.

"Just bring everything in on a tray. I think we'd better have some milk, and cream, and sugar—or maybe honey, if you'd prefer that?" she asked me.

"Sure."

"And some cinnamon. Please use the silver tray. And cloth napkins, please. Not paper."

When Judy opened the door we could see Jack still kneeling there. Jack asked Linda if he could come into the room and join us. She told him no, he had to stay in this position until we left the house, but she said we would keep the door open so he could hear what we were saying. He could listen, but he was not allowed to say anything himself until we were in the car.

Judy brought in the coffee as ordered. She had added some cookies on her own initiative and Linda reprimanded her for this, saying she should have asked permission first. But I told Linda I was in the mood for cookies, so Linda decided not to punish her after all. Meanwhile, as Linda and I sat on the bed eating and drinking and talking about Judy and Jack, Judy sat in her green latex panties at the foot of the bed. At first I felt self-conscious, but I quickly grew to like it. There was something very leisurely about it all, as if I were a pasha. Soon Judy and Jack became invisible. Oddly, this did not make it harder to be with them later, but easier.

Before we left, Judy asked Linda if she could go to the bathroom.

Linda looked at her watch. "No."

"Please. I have to."

"Judy, you asked me and I said no. I don't like to be questioned when I tell you something."

"I'm sorry."

"That's better."

"When am I going to be allowed to go?"

"I'm not sure."

"But I have to go." One leg rubbed against the other.

"Judy, this is very bad." Linda shook her head sadly. "We're going to leave now. In one hour you may call and ask my permission to go to the bathroom. I may pick up my phone or I may have my machine on, I don't know."

"Couldn't she cheat?" I asked Linda in the car.

"What would be the point of that?"

Jack began to explain poopoo sex to me. Sometimes you wouldn't let someone go when they had to, and sometimes you made them go even if they didn't want to, by giving them an enema. After administering the enema, you would forbid them to go—which of course they would be unable not to do—then you would punish them when they did.

This seemed even less like sex than Jack's kneeling outside the door. "Do you do that a lot?" I asked, in the same tone I would ask them if they had seen the latest Bertolucci film.

"Not much," said Linda. "We have enough bathroom problems with my son."

Linda asked me if I had read her article and what I had thought about it. I said it was interesting but a little murky, as if she had been reading too much semiotics. She rolled her eyes at Jack as if I were some philistine.

"Have you heard of Duchess La Jeanne?" Jack asked me.

"No."

"Well, that's Linda's public name. She's the most famous dominatrix in L.A."

That night, despite Jack's docility in kneeling outside Judy's bedroom, he was forced to sleep outside in the dog cage. There was a kind of wall covered by ivy around the property, but there was nothing to prevent a neighbor from peeking through and seeing this, let alone Linda's son. I realized that in peeing all over the bathroom he was not just expressing his displeasure, he was acting like a *dog*. It did rain, and Jack was sniffling the next day. By the time I left for New York a few days later, it had turned into a mild form of pneumonia.

"They say people don't die for love," joked Jack. "But maybe they do."

"I nearly died once of a broken heart," I said. "But I guess that's only a metaphor."

"I take love seriously, but sometimes I wonder if it matters that much who I'm with," said Linda. "Like if Jack died, as horrible as this sounds, I'm sure I'd soon be in love with someone else."

Jack did not seem shocked by this, but I was. Not just that she had said it, but that she had thought it. It was the kind of thing I could imagine myself thinking, though probably not saying, but Linda?

"I often think I don't like people, but when they leave I miss them," I said.

"I never missed my husband when he left," said Linda.

Jack told us about a boy in high school he had had a tremendous crush on. He still regretted not having sex with him, even though he had never slept with a man and had no interest in doing so. He didn't like the idea of having to do stuff with a man's asshole; that was one of the reasons he wasn't into enemas. But women were a different matter. He thought it was a very sexy thing to watch women make love together. That was why he had encouraged Linda and Judy, only it had backfired against him because they never let him join in.

"That doesn't seem fair," I said.

"I think I'll renegotiate it in the next contract," said Jack.

"I don't know about any more contracts," said Linda.

"Is something the matter between you guys?" I asked her the next night. We were driving to The Marquis d'O, a sex club that had a woman's night once a month. Sometimes it was good and lots of sexy people turned up, sometimes it was terrible.

"Well. . .I don't know. In a way I think this relationship has run its course."

"You're not in love with Judy?" I asked.

"Maybe," said Linda. "Sometimes I think I am. She needs me so much."

I thought of mentioning that her children, who needed her too, did not seem to receive much of the benefits of Linda's empathy. "What about Jack? He seems to need you too."

"I know," she sighed. "That's the problem." She paused. "Jack'll be okay. I'll always be there for him. He knows that."

"Are you really the most famous dominatrix in LA?" I asked.

"Yes. It's a great way for people like us to make money and not have it interfere with their art. You make a hundred dollars an hour, sometimes more—not including tips."

"What do you have to do?"

"Insults, dressing up, enemas, spankings. You negotiate with the customer. If it's something really disgusting, I won't do it."

"I can't believe it, Linda," I said. "I still think of you as a nice Jewish girl."

"I *am* a nice Jewish girl. Don't you think you're a little naive?" We pulled into the parking place.

"Tsk," Linda said, that sound of the tongue between the teeth. Only ten or twelve women were in the club, which smelled of old liquor and cigarettes. A fat woman dressed in a black leather slip and halter stood behind the bar. She gave Linda and me free drinks. Everyone seemed to know Linda. The women were incredibly unattractive, overweight or unduly skinny, with pale unhealthy-looking skin—unless this was due to the lighting, which seemed designed to make everyone look like heroin addicts. They were dressed in predictable ways: black leather pants, belts studded with silver, metal bracelets around their wrists. The conventionality of style and fantasy with which people into this form of sex expressed their violations of conventionality has always been astonishing to me. A few women were dressed in classic pornography style, with tight little skirts and lacy black camisoles or bras. One had on just a bra and g-string with garters and stockings.

Several wore dog collars around their necks attached to leather leashes wound around their mistresses' wrists. They stood by passively with pouty lips and expressionless eyes as their owners opened their shirts and fondled their breasts in public. Sometimes their breasts or buttocks were offered to other women to touch, and when this was done they evinced no reaction either. Linda was popular, and everybody offered her their slaves. As she stroked them she would talk about them in the third person, telling the person who had given her permission to touch them how attractive, how soft, how obedient their slaves were.

"If you'd like, I could ask permission for you to touch somebody too", Linda said.

"No thanks."

"Are you scared?"

"No. They're too ugly." What bothered me even more than their looks was their apparent social class—rather, their apparent lack of social class. They looked like they lived in East L.A., or some cheap place in the Valley.

We went into the back room where the action, if any, usually took place. The walls were black, and as it was lit by only a dim red lamp it took me a few seconds to see what was going on. There were several sets of stocks—the kind Puritans used to punish sinners, with holes to secure the head and hands—and some basket-like leather seats hung on chains from the ceiling. On a shelf in the rear was your standard assortment of paddles, whips, riding crops.

A woman was standing on a little platform, her bottom naked, her head and hands held in place by the stock. She was surrounded by several women who took turns swatting her with a whip. There was no urgency to this, minutes seeming to go by between each stroke. One woman always stood by the head of the woman being whipped, stroking her brow, pushing her hair off her forehead, wiping off the sweat, talking to her through the moans and telling her how beautiful and sweet and responsive she was.

We watched for a while, then the woman holding the whip offered it to me. I would have preferred to just watch but Linda had told me that if anyone asked me to do something I should do it; if I refused to participate I would make everyone uncomfortable, perhaps might even be asked to leave. Women were still a little touchy about this kind of sex, it had a very bad name—not just in the world but in the women's and even the lesbian movement. It was the big philosophical issue at the moment. Surely I must have read the articles.

"Actually, I don't buy that kind of magazine."

"You should. This kind of sex is really the last frontier. Dealing with this is just as difficult as coming out."

"I didn't know you were out," I had said to Linda.

Feeling curious, but not the least sexual, I took the whip. It had a nice, balanced feel. I raised my arm, then flicked it rather gently. You could barely hear the whip land on the woman's ass.

"You can do it harder," she said.

I tried again. Again, it was too gentle.

"Do it harder," the other women told me. "Don't be afraid of hurting her." *Harder*: the word sounded odd in their mouths.

After a few more strokes I began to get into it, and the woman I was hitting began to moan and say "ow." It was gratifying, though not immensely so. Soon an empathy—for the pain I was inflicting on her and the connection we were making through it—began to manifest itself in my body, so that I had my first flickerings of arousal. I no longer cared that she wasn't attractive, and the idea of running my hand over her face or caressing her breast no longer seemed so revolting.

After a while I was told to give the whip to someone else. I was about to leave the room when Linda grabbed my arm.

"Now you," she said.

"What?"

"You want to," she said. "I can tell."

"No."

"Ha!" She began to stroke my thighs. I'm not attracted to Linda, but I felt this searing flash go through me. Then her hand moved to my crotch. "I can feel the heat through your pants."

"Linda. . ." I pushed her hand away.

She grabbed my arms and pinned me against a wall near where we were standing. She was strong, but perhaps if I had really tried I could have pushed her away. But I shut my eyes and let her continue to caress me.

"You want me to, don't you?"

"No."

She laughed. "You sure fooled me."

"Not here."

"What's wrong with here?"

I leaned forward to whisper in her ear. "For one thing, the women are so ugly."

"They're not so bad," said Linda. "What about the one over there, you don't think she's attractive?"

"No."

"Or her?"

"No. I can honestly say there's not one person in this place I feel like having sex with," I said. Then I realized I might be insulting Linda. "I mean, not counting you. You're my friend." Then I realized Linda might be thinking I was making a pass at her, so I added. "Not that I'm attracted to you. God, you know what I mean, it's too complicated to explain."

"It's what you do that's important, not necessarily the people you do it with," said Linda. "You have very nice legs," she said, still stroking me. "Why don't you relax and see what happens?"

"I can't. Not in public."

"But you're wet, I can feel it," she said. "Will it be easier if I put a blindfold around your eyes so you don't have to see what's happening?" She touched my breast.

"Okay," I whispered.

"Wait a minute. I'll be right back."

I stood there, self-conscious, as if she were still propping me up, my eyes shut so I could not see the other women who might be looking at me.

"I don't want you to open your eyes, but move your head forward a bit," said Linda. I moved my head forward and she slipped a blindfold over my head. "Is that better?" she asked.

"Yes."

"Now I want you to unzip your pants."

"I can't do that."

"You have to," she said.

I unzipped my pants. I felt foolish with them slightly open, and did not know whether I should push them down more or not. I didn't want to ask because that would look too eager. I almost wished my hands were tied so I would not have to worry about these things.

"Now I'm going to take you by the hand and lead you someplace where you'll be a little more comfortable."

"I'm scared my pants are going to fall down and I'll trip."

"Hold my hand and you'll be all right."

We walked a number of steps, then she told me to stop. She pushed my pants down so they were around my ankles. I couldn't remember what underpants I had worn that day and I was worried they had holes in them, or the crotch was pinkish-brown from blood I hadn't quite been able to wash out from my period. I told myself it was dark in the room and they wouldn't be able to see my underpants anyway. Then I began to worry that maybe she had brought me to the other room.

"We're still in the back room, aren't we?" I asked Linda.

"Relax," said Linda.

"I don't want to be up front. People might recognize me."

"This is a very safe environment," said Linda. "Whoever's here is only going to deal with you with love. Now I want you to lean over."

"But I'll fall!"

"No. There's something here. You'll be more comfortable."

I was draped over an object that felt like a pommel horse. It was covered with suede and had many smells in it. My mouth lay against it but I tried not to touch it with my lips so I would not catch the diseases that were surely nesting there. I was scared I was going to sneeze or have to blow my nose or even pee.

Linda began stroking my thighs. She began telling me how beautiful I was, how soft and compliant. I spread my legs a little so she could touch between them, though I did it in a way that I hoped would look like I was just shifting my weight. "Oh, that's nice," she said. She touched the bottom of my underpants. "You're incredibly wet," she said. "Do you know that? . . . I said, do you know that?" I nodded. "Now I want you to lift yourself up a little. . ." She raised me off the horse and pulled down my underpants. She ran her fingers up the backs of my thighs again, then began to lightly touch my ass. "What a pretty ass she has," she said. "Isn't this a pretty ass? See how it moves towards me when I touch it." And it did; I couldn't help myself, although whether it was because I was so turned on or because I was being hypnotized by her commands I was unable to tell. Now that Linda was talking about me in the third person the fact that I was in a club returned to the forefront of my attention and I realized there was a hum of voices around us and that they had been there for some time; I had just blocked them out. They were talking about me in the same calm tones they had used a little earlier in talking about the girl who had been in the stocks— how sweet and docile and vulnerable I looked lying there, how pretty my ass was and how it would look even prettier the next day when it was black-and-blue. "Go ahead, touch her, she doesn't mind," said Linda, and I felt the hands of strangers, the different hands of strangers, moving up my thighs and caressing my ass. Occasionally they would just brush by my crotch.

"She's really wet," they said.

"She's cherry," explained Linda.

"Oh, this is your first time," one said to me. I tried to nod, but it was difficult in the position I was in. She put her hand on my neck and gently stroked it. "We know how you feel," she said. It was very soothing. "Don't worry. We won't do anything you don't want. You know that, don't you?" I tried to nod again, but she kept talking, and I realized she wasn't doing this so much to get an answer as to soothe me by the sound of her voice. I felt soothed. It was really very nice to be talked about like that, in such complimentary tones, in a way that I was not usually talked about unless I had done something extraordinarily witty or wonderful. But for once nothing seemed to be expected of me except to lie there.

I felt a sting across my ass. I assumed it was Linda's hand. I said "ow," more out of surprise than pain. My thighs were stroked again, and I trembled, waiting for the stroke. When it didn't come I was almost disappointed. I twitched my ass.

"See how she wants it," said someone.

"Oh yes. She's quite the little femme."

Again I felt the hand. It hurt more this time but I was expecting it and I didn't say anything. A finger tickled the hair in my ass, then slid down to my crotch.

"She's very wet."

"She'd probably beg for it if we stopped."

"You could tell she was that way when she walked in."

"People who act tough are always the biggest femmes."

"Ow!" I said. This time the hand really hurt. Then the spanks began to come more quickly. I realized my "ows" were due not so much to the intensity of the strokes as to their unpredictability. In a way I wanted to keep saying ow," to let them know they were hurting me, but I didn't want to say it too much, in case they would stop. Then I thought about how crazy it was that even in here, when everything was being done for my pleasure, all I could think about was what kind of response I was supposed to make. Was there never a moment in my entire life when I could just relax?

I don't know whether it was the lecture or the hypnotic rhythm of the strokes, but after a while my mind stopped its chattering, and I was in a different kind of space, the one that exists while you're in a dream or watching a totally engrossing movie, and there's nothing to do but calmly witness the events going on all around you.

It was totally peaceful. I wanted to go to sleep. When they stopped I felt bereft, as if I had been chucked out of paradise.

"You can go on," I told Linda. "I'm okay."

"You've had enough."

She removed the blindfold, and I was forced to look at the women around me. They were still ugly, and though I felt more empathy for them than I had before, I wasn't sure whether this made it better or worse.

The next day I felt terribly depressed. I wanted to expunge my thoughts in water but the blue marks on my ass and thighs made me too embarrassed to go to the health club and swim. When Linda went to visit Judy I realized I was jealous—not of either of them but of the acts that went on between them. I knew on my own I would not have the courage to do such things. I lay in bed most of the day and slept, then I took the red-eye home.

I hadn't talked to Linda for almost a year when I received a creamy, engraved, stiff card inside a creamy, engraved, stiff envelope informing me that the former Ms. Linda Birnbaum of Westwood and Dr. Henry Goldberg of Beverly Hills were pleased to announce their marriage. The receipt of this note made it safe for me to contact Linda again. In the course of the conversation I asked her if she had shared the details of her life as Duchess La Jeanne with her new husband.

"Oh no," she said. "I stopped that stuff when Jack and I broke up, soon after you were here. I realized it wasn't me at all." She told me that her son had stopped peeing all over the bathroom soon after Jack had moved out and that, as there was currently no extra room in Henry's house, her sculpture was temporarily on hold until they could build her a studio in his garage. One other thing. Henry had no children, and she was trying to get pregnant. At her age this was difficult, and she went into a long litany about bilirubins and luteal phase deficiencies and b.b.t. curves. It was both boring and reassuring, and served exactly the same conversational function as discussions of one's latest therapy session had in the old days.

When I hung up the phone I was both relieved and disappointed to discover I had been right, that deep down Linda was, as I had always thought, a nice Jewish girl. I realized also that, for some reason, no matter what I did or did not do, I was not, and this both relieved and disappointed me too.

from **Don Juan in the Village**

The Kiss

"Two days in a row, I'm honored," Miss Maxfeld said, when she opened her door to find me standing there.

"I was just walking around and thought I'd drop by and say hello," I said.

"You hung up on me on the telephone a little while ago, didn't you?" she asked.

"Don't be silly. Why would I do that?"

"You tell me. But only a fool wouldn't know when you're lying—your eyes shift down and your face gets red. How you ever manage to fool your parents is beyond me."

"I told you, they're idiots. I thought you were leaving school early," I accused her, to distract her from the question of my veracity.

"I *did* leave early. I had to take care of some business at the bank, and then once I got out of the bank I decided I might as well do all my other errands—so I stopped at the cleaners and picked up two skirts, and then I went to the laundry. But the laundry wasn't ready and the delivery boy didn't show up today, so I'll have to go down later and pick it up myself. But, my dear, surely none of this is of great interest to you. Come in and sit down."

Actually, I didn't find it all that tedious: in the mood I was in there was something comforting about the inanity of daily life. "I'm all right," I told her, still standing with my books by the door.

"You were walking around; that doesn't sound like you," she continued. "You always claim you find it so boring."

"It *was* boring. I went to the zoo for a while. This guard told me how he hated the animals. Then this creep exposed himself to me. It was really disgusting." I paused. There was something else. I had rehearsed my litany of the day so that I'd be able to make conversation. "Oh, yeah, and I almost froze to death too."

"How dramatic! You make it sound like Lancelot searching for the Holy Grail."

"Very funny. If you can tell me about *your* day, I can tell you about *mine*."

"I take it you weren't accompanied by your customary gaggle of sycophants?" (It was how she'd referred to the girls who hung around the Plaza hotel hoping John or Paul or even George or Ringo would notice them.)

"All by my lonesome."

"No wonder you're feeling sorry for yourself."

"I'm *not* feeling sorry for myself. I'm cold and I'm tired and I couldn't sleep last night, that's all."

"Then stop standing by the door and come sit down."

"I don't know." I shrugged. For some reason I was finding it difficult to move.

"Ever since I've known you, you've been telling me you can't sleep at night," she said.

"This was different." It was a perfect opportunity for her to ask me *how* it was different, but she didn't.

"You're always *saying* it's different, but it always sounds exactly the same."

"Are you trying to tell me I bore you?" I asked. This was my greatest fear about everyone.

"Of course not, my dear, every quiver of your feverish sensibility holds me in thrall."

"Ha ha. I *am* boring you. Maybe I should leave." I switched my books from one hand to the other.

"Don't be silly. You just got here. At least take off your wet shoes and let me make you some tea."

"What's the point? I have to go outside in a few minutes, and I'll just get cold all over again."

"Honestly, Lynn, I don't think I've ever met anybody who was so determined to be miserable."

"Like I always said, I'm unique."

"You *are* unique, dear, but not in the way you think."

Usually this form of flattery pleased me, but today it made me feel even worse—that the con I tried to put over on everybody about how I was interesting and intelligent (when I was really the most boring person who had ever lived) was working even on her: was there anybody in the world who knew what I was really like? But I knew I'd feel even more depressed if I left, so, still holding my books, I walked over to the window while she put on the water. Up three flights of fire escape, almost level to us, two men sat in profile across a table, apparently engaged in earnest discussion. A piece of toast popped up. Two pieces. After the toast was buttered, the one who was not wearing glasses put on his glasses, and they both picked up books and started reading. Then I became aware of the ticking of the kitchen clock.

"You look very unhappy," Miss Maxfeld said.

"What do I have to be unhappy about?"

"Things without number, I'm sure. And none of them terribly important, as you'll realize someday, someday not very far off."

"I suppose you're going to tell me 'Youth is wasted on the young.' God! I might as well be talking to my father. As if it's the least bit reassuring to be told that everything that's bothering you is trivial. You don't even have any idea of what's going through my mind."

"Then why don't you tell me? Though I have an idea I already know." I didn't know which was more plausible—that she did or she didn't: of course she *had* to, but if she *did*, how could she stand my nauseating presence in her house? As she stared at me, I looked away—at the floor, at the ceiling, through the wall—so she wouldn't see me blush. But it seemed so obvious an evasion I couldn't stand it, so I walked to the door. "I don't think we should see each other anymore," I said.

"If you think it's best, of course not. But is that really what you want?" I couldn't tell if she was trying to find out what I really wanted or trying to tell me what *she* really wanted (or perhaps they were the same).

"Mr. Pauley's a homosexual, isn't he?" I heard myself ask.

"Even if he were, do you think I'd tell you?"

"That sounds like a yes."

"It's not Mr. Pauley you're really curious about, is it?"

What I really wanted was to walk out the door so I wouldn't have to find out the answer to my unspoken question. "I don't know," I answered. Tears came to my eyes as they had in the zoo and downstairs earlier while I'd waited for her in the hall.

"Of course you know," she said. Then she did what I suddenly realized I had expected her to do during all of that long year: to place her hands on the shoulders of my coat and straighten my lapels, and lift me up so that the heels of my Village Cobbler shoes rose off the floor. Then she kissed me on the lips. (She did *not*, however, stick her tongue in my mouth.) Then she released her hands from my coat and lowered me down.

I didn't know what to do, so I stood there like a statue, but a statue with human self-consciousness.

"Wait a second," she said, "I'll be right back." She disappeared into the bedroom and returned with a tissue and a sweater. I blew my nose and stuffed the tissue in my pocket, then I took off the coat and put on the sweater. "Don't forget. There's a paper due tomorrow. Comparing Coleridge and Wordsworth."

"Oh, no. Well. . .thanks for the tea."

"Lynn, you didn't *have* any tea."

"Oh, no. Well. *Thanks."*

"Thank you."

Waiting for the bus, I tried to figure out if what had seemed to happen had actually happened, or whether, out of the combination of desire and longing I had felt all year, I had created the hallucination of a Kiss. Even if I had not created the hallucination of a Kiss, perhaps I was "projecting" sexual intent onto the kind of friendly embrace Shelley, for instance, might have given me (had Shelley been friendly).

Intuition told me the Kiss (assuming, for the moment, there had been a Kiss) was sexual: although not a "soul kiss," its duration and intensity were such that, had a boy been doing it to me, I would have been surprised had he not tried to progress through at least several (if not all) of the remaining categories on the Purity Test. But Reason told me Intuition had been wrong many times this year: night after night I had been absolutely convinced I couldn't breathe and was about to die-but I could, and I hadn't. (But Kennedy *had;* "deader than a mackerel" as Wolf had chortled, more than once.)

Reason told me it was impossible a teacher of mine should place his/her lips on mine for any reason whatsoever (sexual or non) and yet this had happened (unless I was crazy).

(Even if I was crazy, this *still* could have happened: it just made it less likely that anybody—including myself—would believe it.)

Miss Maxfeld's kiss seemed no more plausible than Leonard's arm falling off in my hand, in what I was almost certain had been a dream (unless the dream world were the real, and this real one the dream), but it was only Reason which had been surprised by the Kiss: Intuition had known it was coming (or rather, when it had come, Intuition realized it had not been surprised).

My lack of surprise was the only surprise.

Wasn't this the mark of an insane person—to accept the anomalies of life (trees that cried, people floating through air, birds who talked Greek) as natural phenomena—rather than the creations of a disturbed mind? Was the insanity the hallucination (which, after all, occurred to everybody), or rather the calm acceptance of them?

I got onto the bus, which might not be there (if I were insane), and showed the driver my bus pass, and pushed my way to the rear, thereby stepping on the toes of a little girl who was almost surely there (for she kicked me back). *"Ow,"* I said. *"Hey."*

"Jennifer, you stop that this instant," said her mother. "I don't know what's with you today." The mother sighed, and Jennifer gave me a vicious smirk, the kind I might have given her, had our positions been reversed. She had long blond hair and blue eyes, and wore the kind of navy blue jumper and white shirt that certain of the more upper-class Episcopalian and Catholic private schools demanded. She was between the ages of eight and eleven, depending on whether she was small or large for her age. I realized I envied her: not just for her blond hair but for her school uniform, her religion, her mother.

Relatively gently (so I wouldn't permanently injure her) but quite purposefully, I kicked her back.

She watched me doing this, and her eyes opened in shock. I winked. "That girl's kicking me," she told her mother.

"I'm warning you, Jennifer," her mother told her. She wiped a strand of pale brown (or dark blond) hair out of her own blue eyes, then said to me: "I'm terribly sorry, I don't know what's come over her today. She's been acting like this all afternoon."

"She was *kicking* me," Jennifer repeated, in a voice more outraged this time (due to her mother's disbelief). I would have kicked her again, thereby linking us even more closely in our strange game, had an old man on the seat beside where I was standing not begun staring at me. I stared back at his eyes, then down at my feet, to show him what a selfish fart he was for not offering me his seat. He stretched out his hand and massaged his leg, sighed, then he put his hand to his neck and started massaging that too. As the bus swung out into traffic, I leaned into his body to show him I wasn't impressed by his "headache," then straightened myself by pushing against his arm (with a little more force than was strictly necessary). The little girl continued to watch me distrustfully. Noticing this, I winked again.

"Mommy, she's hitting that old man," the girl told her mother.

The mother gave an exaggerated sigh, looked out the window, offered me an apologetic (but also somewhat hostile) smile, then dragged the little girl to the rear of the bus. She found a seat and parked the girl in it, then stood in front of her so she couldn't escape. "For the last time I'm warning you. . ." I heard the familiar line, the "music of childhood" Miss Maxfeld had said (about some other phrase, I couldn't remember at the moment what it was).

I wondered what the mother of the little girl would do if I told her a female teacher thirty-seven years of age with a mustache had just kissed me on the lips. Probably she would think she had not heard me correctly, that she was having an aural hallucination, but no doubt she would remove her child from the bus (just to make *sure),* and for some reason she would tend to believe her child's story as to who had been kicking whom—even though my statement should have induced her to accept anything I said, because what liar would make up such a shameful, disgusting, and illegal tale? Or she might think that she had heard me correctly, and that I was insane, but still she would remove her child from the bus, in case I should be overcome by an "irresistible impulse" (the kind that made Leopold and Loeb murder Loeb's younger cousin) and start to brush the hair out of her daughter's bright blue eyes, and tell her to be the happy child I had never been.

I would not have thought yesterday (or this morning) I could do such a thing, but today Miss Maxfeld had kissed me on the lips (if, indeed, she *had* kissed me on the lips), and that made all things possible.

I wondered whether Miss Maxfeld had always been a female homosexual, or if it had been my presence that aroused the irresistible impulse in her, the sight of my blue ("blue" as in "unhappy") eyes under my brown hair.

The full implication of my thoughts struck me, and I pulled the cord to stop the bus, so I could get off at the next stop, to save myself and the little girl from this same possible irresistible impulse in me.

I had been an official female homosexual for less than twenty minutes, and already I had become a dangerous person. ("So like you, to sneak up on me unawares," Miss Maxfeld had said.) I remembered all her sayings because I had repeated them to myself so many times in the last months (whether to lull myself to sleep or keep me awake, I was not sure).

I knew I was a homosexual because a woman had kissed me on the lips (if I wasn't crazy, if I wasn't lying).

In my depression I took a taxi home. My parents would scream at me if they caught me doing this—a terrible waste of money whenever you did it—but even more so at this hour of the day, when it was necessary not for safety or even convenience but to save time. (Time, for my parents, was not money.) ("You can buy anything *but* time," said Leonard, calling up a limousine to take him to the airport.)

I felt a certain grim satisfaction at this further instance of my degeneracy. Now that a woman had kissed me, there was nothing I might not do: rob a bank, become a prostitute, buy caviar.

When I got home, I went into the bathroom, shut the door, pulled the hand towel my mother kept *in* the sink (so that the water dripping out of the faucet would not turn the sink blue) *out* of the sink, turned on the tap, let it run, turned it off, replaced the hand towel back in the sink, and flushed the toilet—partly for the noise but mostly so that I could watch the water swirl counterclockwise down, as it does in North America. I wished I were going down with it, all the way to Rio de Janeiro, where it would swirl the other way.

My mother kept a towel in the sink so the sink wouldn't get wet—and *I* was the one who was considered crazy! (*Every*body in *every* family is crazy.)

I opened the medicine chest, took out the little metal tube with the white cream I had seen spread over my mother's lip, and read: "Doctors approve this safe and easy-to-use method of removing unsightly and unwanted hair growth efficiently and safely. Instructions on other side. Discontinue at slightest sign of irritation. It is suggested that the user test ointment on leg before proceeding to use on the face." Even when I was young, I had known the use of a facial depilatory was embarrassing, something one should not discuss—like one's period, or the smell of one's friends when they had *their* period.

Men shaved, but that was different. You could discuss it on the radio if you felt like it, if you were ever on the radio.

I stared at the hairless area above my lip. It might stay that way forever, or I might grow a mustache tomorrow. Even if I didn't grow one for years, I could never be sure that one would never appear, any more than I could ever be sure that the next breathing spell might not be real, and I would die.

I wondered if Miss Maxfeld's Kiss (assuming it had occurred) had accelerated the development of my mustache, like a hormone. I wondered if her mustache would tickle me the next time we kissed, *if* we kissed a next time, *if* we had (indeed) kissed a first time.

If we kissed a next time, I could be almost positive that we had kissed a first time. But even if she never kissed me again, I could never be sure we hadn't kissed a first time, for it might be ignored, the way so many odd occurrences were ignored by my family: Leonard's multiple residences, the fact that Aunt Lou was a virgin, my mother's mustache.

If Miss Maxfeld had not kissed me on the lips, then I was not necessarily a lesbian.

Inside, however, I felt like one. In fact, I felt like I had felt like one my whole life. The only surprise was that I had not noticed this sooner.

Then it seemed to me I *had* noticed this sooner—noticed it all year, in fact, in the midst of my awful longing for Miss Maxfeld ("awful" in the sense not just of "terrible" and "unpleasant," but "inspiring awe")—I just hadn't put a name to it.

But what was "it"—this sense of newness—if *not* a name? I was, after all, the same person I had always been. *(Wasn't I?)*

And yet, though I was not surprised to be a lesbian, it did not seem possible I could be one, for surely God had intended me to be perfect. It could not be that in the one life I would lead on earth, I was to be permanently and irrevocably marred.

I had already been kissed, and I was already irrevocably marred. Nothing on earth could erase the fact that I had been kissed by a homosexual woman—not unless I had a lobotomy. (Even then, this wouldn't erase the *fact*—just the memory.)

If what had happened today had indeed happened, then the notion of destiny I had read about in novels was wrong, for it was not Fate but only an amazing and improbable coincidence that the *only* other homosexual woman I knew *in the whole* world had put her lips on mine! How could such an anomaly possibly have anything to do with me?

I was *drenched* in anomaly, for in all probability I knew three homosexual people (Miss Maxfeld, Mr. Pauley, and

Rudolf), four if you counted myself. I was only sixteen, and already I knew more homosexuals than my father said he had ever met in his whole life.

If *I* was drenched in anomaly, just think of my high school, in which a minimum of three people (out of a thousand) were homosexual (me, Miss Maxfeld, and Mr. Pauley). If you extrapolated that figure to the country as a whole, that would mean there were six hundred thousand homosexuals in the United States of America alone—not counting the rest of the world! This was so much anomaly, that maybe (after all) it *was* Fate.

from ***In Thrall***

Patient Zero

1

Flying was the best. Doing nothing you went somewhere. It was noisy but behind the noise there was silence, up there where words meant nothing. It was the sky, white and pink and gold and blue, the clouds puffy like sheep in the pictures of heaven in the books about the Bible he had been given as a child. Where God was a wise old man with a beard and everybody got what they deserved and you almost forgot you had to be dead to be there.

He handed them their meals, the rich old men and the rich young men. Sometimes he gossiped and sometimes he flirted and sometimes he pretended he was a statue, beautiful and white and cold and absolutely impervious to the touch. Even though he was the server he conveyed a look that even though they were there in business or first class and he was earning dip in some way they weren't as good as him. Because he believed it they believed it. He sensed it in the way they handed back their trays, the jokes they tried to make when they saw him undressing them in his mind. They didn't know why. But it disturbed them.

Ostentatiously he ran his eyes down their zippers. He could stare so long the idea of it would bring an erection. Sometimes, then, he'd avert his eyes in disgust.

Not because he was disgusted. But to show them that although he was the server, in the real life the story was very different than that.

The silver wings mirrored sun into the eyes like the water below the cliffs at Newport Beach. He had been there with a rich man who owned a red Aston-Martin and bought him a $180 pair of Italian sunglasses. It had occurred to him that if he so chose he could very easily end up living in Newport Beach, having a free rein at that red Aston-Martin. The man was 47 and unduly proud of his body.

The night was filled with tiny pricks of light, like the cigarettes in the collapsing building down by the water in New York where his relationships were brief but intense. As much as he wished for the Aston-Martin he felt happier among the rotting floorboards. He strutted there like a king bestowing favors on his servants.

2

He rides the subway. He has no money. He gets off at East 19th Street, Broadway IRT, heads downtown to the Baths. He stops at a newsstand to scan the headlines on a paper he will not bother to buy. Reagan has been shot. His smiling face on the covers. Gaetan likes him. He is a conservative, of French extraction. If someone brings the subject up, he will probably agree that Quebec should secede from the rest of Canada, though he has no interest in how this might be done and certainly none in contributing to it himself.

He likes trouble. He likes chaos. He likes things being

nowhere. He likes being nowhere, in an airplane, over everything, between here and there, the realm of infinite possibility. It's not infinite of course, but people much more intelligent and thoughtful and possessing more taste than him speak and perhaps even think in such cliches. "The realm of infinite possibility," he thinks, as he parades in front of a series of half-open doors, of men illuminated by bare bulbs or sometimes not at all, and it does not always happen that he will turn to the beautiful body, because the beautiful body is not always as interesting as the ugly body, even more so the unknown body, the body that is almost assuredly ugly but sometimes is not, waiting for a body in the dark.

3

Of course he has thought of murder. You who have wished your spouse or your children to disappear, your parents, surely can understand why he would like to murder the irritatingly compliant stranger who is so willing to service him in whatever way he wishes to be serviced, who, because God or Fate or Genes made his features comely, his hair blond, his eyes blue, a twinkle in them, dimples, means that thousands of strangers are upon a demi-second acquaintance willing to let his member penetrate both ends of their digestive systems, be willing to enfold his sperm (encoded variously with gonorrhea bacteria, syphilis, herpes, hepatitis B virus amongst others known & unknown) into the sensitive absorbent tissues of their anuses or mouths, be willing to insert their tongue into these openings, exchanging saliva, licking droplets of urine (salt, safer than saliva), shit—bad breath, disease, torn sphincter muscles, pain. They will let him wrap his belt around their neck and squeeze (how hard to stop—but not to do so would, if not this day, this bathhouse, then the next or the next, indirectly cause the ending of this pleasure—but then there would be prison and *its* pleasures—he thinks of this, too, with pleasure), they will let him decorate their bodies with the blacks and reds and blues of the struck body areas swelling with blood following the application of a blow/lash/whip, etc. He loves and hates them for this, as he has (when ill with the aftereffects of too many people, drugs, places) on occasion hated himself, for brief periods of time, until the headache wears off.

The infections he bears with grace and humor. He boasts of them to the doctor: "I should buy my penicillin wholesale." He regales the black nurse with tales of his many bouts with gonorrhea, syphilis, amebiasis, hepatitis B and its relapses, the many times he has sat in a coffee shop on East 70th Street in NY (or Toronto or LA) eating three eggs and bacon, toast, coffee, lots of coffee, then going upstairs to the waiting room where he drinks the stuff to make him shit, then waits, and waits, reading *Time* & *Newsweek*, desultorily (this is not a sexy place) eying the men (women don't do such disgusting things to one another), trying to shit, drinking more coffee. The bathroom smells, mostly of meat molecules mingled in air, but other things too, as does the waiting room itself. How can it not, seeing this is a place devoted exclusively to *shit*—the expulsion & analysis thereof. He starts to cough, retch, instinctively props himself with his hands against the bowl. Instinctively wiping the sweat with those hands he retches more, washes his hands, washes the faucet with his hands, washes his hands again, grabs the towel that has been touched. They're out of paper towels, he tells the nurse. Again.

He will wait while they search his shit for. . .not worms, exactly, but amoeba. . .tiny one-celled animals through a microscope lens. They are hard to spot, not distributed equally in every piece of the dark brown detritus (as stars supposedly are in the empyrean), not even in every batch. If the diarrhea continues, the vague pains, it could be anything, but in a month or two he might have to do the eggs/bacon routine again. Nor does the medicine always work. The inside of his digestive track, this place that connects one end of the food chain to another, is hospitable to organisms of all sorts, and he is a generous host. He never shuts the door on them, even when he is tired, or ill, or has to keep excusing himself to go to the bathroom. He is compulsively hospitable. Anyone can have him, go anywhere they want in his body. He is too nice and cannot say no. He takes pity on strangers. He is a paragon of virtues—Gallic charm, American friendliness, English tactfulness. He comes back for the medicine again and again and again.

A door opens. A large pot of half-drunk coffee, almost the same color as the detritus, sits on a table. The same pot men in the waiting room (no—women do not do such disgusting things to their bodies) get their coffee from. Two people in white coats sit on stools, an eye of each on a round black lens, a microscope. A young black man wearing glasses, jeans beneath the lab coat. A white woman in her 30s, 40s. The room is small, with a tiny frosted window, no bathroom. The black man looks up and sees him, a neutral gaze. Is he straight? This job is less well-paid than you might think.

"What's your name?" the receptionist asks.

"Gaetan. Gaetan Dugas."

4

He is walking on the pier, a cold November night. Not too many people. It is cold. Not like summer. Some clouds, white-rimmed, his ass has golden hair, rimmed (by whites, usually, but sometimes blacks). Well, the hair is not golden but it is not black so it is golden. People like this. They like his body that never gets tanned, even when he lies naked on a wooden deck in a house in Malibu, gin-&-tonic by his side, a Quaalude and dexedrene/s in his stomach, like a car, a pig being roasted, a condom entering a nervous digestive track. He lies stretched in the sun all day, barely waking to be fucked (he glances at the comics). At the end of the day he is barely red. The man is older, a doctor, shrink but also medical (hence the incredible array of uppers & downers), not exactly paying him but Gaetan gets the best—smoked salmon, caviar, etc. he is only sorry he cannot think of more expensive things, there is a limit to what one can spend on food. He buys Gaetan a jacket from one of the famous Italian designers, almost as soft as a woman's glove, dark brown in color (same as the stuff under the microscope), & some shirts. A nylon (leather is too heavy) bag for Gaetan to stuff them in.

The doctor has a friend, a shrink to the stars. They tell x-rated, confidential stories about people well-known to most Americans. Some of these stories Gaetan has heard before, archetypes of lust and perversion joked about in bathhouses and bars from coast to coast; others sad tales of the the doctors' disappointment in gardeners, butlers, tennis pros, cooks. The doctors sound bored, like Gaetan, and as usual he thinks "there is no difference between them and me." Surely Gaetan has looks and charisma; thousands from coast to coast, from the chill of Saskatchewan to the winds of Holland to the warmth of Honolulu can attest to this. Also: Goa, Cairo, Tokyo, Helsinki. Moscow. Roma, Warszawa. He should be up there on screen; he will get to it one of these days. You cannot take acting lessons when you are a steward. The job has many perks but continuity is not one of them. He has been screen-tested more than once; perhaps as a seduction ploy. These men did not call him back. Half in envy, eyes closed, orange against his lids, the doctors laugh and gossip. Vaguely amusing at first, the more he listens the less so it becomes, the further away his hosts seem, the more pathetic the famous actress, the actor with the tiny penis, the endless stream of "chauffeurs" and "masseurs" and "physical trainers," the more irritating the drunken laughing doctors, the less inclined he feels towards coke and more towards Quaaludes, he gets on a rubber raft with his gin and lies, face up, too lazy to swim, dragging feet in the water, kicking it against the side of the pool, drifting away from the voices. . . He wakes up to his cock being sucked. This is okay, but it is not happening to him.

5

"The Spot." Dick, Jane, and Spot the Dog. *Richard, Jeanne, et 'Petit Ennui' le chien*? The name that is silly, more generic than name, makes it friendly, okay. Deathly afraid of skin cancer (although he doesn't burn—but perhaps that's *worse*), he puts off going to the doctor. But it gets bigger and then there is another. So nervous he sweats and he cannot sleep, he confides in a friend. The friend sets up a drink with his friend, a receptionist in the office of a skin doctor who advertises on the subway, who assures him the purple spot is not melanoma.

But what is it, doc? Dunno.

He sleeps somewhat better the next few nights, then the sweats and insomnia returns. "I should go to a real doctor," he thinks. Then he meets someone in Athens and forgets all about this.

6

He has his disappointments, too, his rejections. A boy in _____ a man in _____ He loved a businessman once, who knocked off famous perfumes by using a computer to exhaustively analyze the contents. There was a young boy, a Tunisian. He had a girlfriend here he was going to marry if his family let him, she was not Muslim. It was not the best sex, but the most passion—the brother, perhaps, he never had. When he left to visit his family in Tunis, he sent Gaetan a few letters, boring, short, the kind you might write to anyone. He's supposed to come back, but never does. Gaetan finagles a flight to Tunis, tries to find the boy's home, but nobody can read the address. Someone finally takes him to a large office building. He enters the lobby. It is a bank. Across the street he sits in a cafe, but recognizes no one. Rather, everyone looks half-familiar. They have the same names too—"Abdul," "Mohammed"—he is not sure if it matters, one Abdul or the other, as long as he is young, with laughing dark eyes, fine smooth skin. But perhaps it does, for his encounters there do not especially satisfy him, and he gets (also gives, surely) the clap, and his wallet is stolen. The sun bothers him too, another spot appears.

7

Blue sky. Outer space. Empyrean. Heaven. Night. Day. Clouds. Plate. Rain. Sun. Dawn. Snow. Engine. Lightning. Bathroom. Water. Movie. Life vest. Chicken. Nutra-sweet. Iceberg lettuce. Ice. More ice. Galley. Busy. Delayed. Mississippi. Emergency exit. Wing.

8

(Later.) Beauty. Buoyancy. Life vest. Sun. Landing. Amaretto. Youth. Check. Hotel. Balcony.

9

The doctor takes his blood pressure, pulse. Lots of blood. Urine. Stool. He is to come back next week. There is something wrong, perhaps. The night sweats are definitely worse. He must change his shirt, several times a night, like a menopausal woman.

He is walking in the park. He eyes the vendor of hot dogs, almost forty, Latin, slipping the fetish shape into the warmed bun, with disgust. Only the young can be poor. The old must be not just wealthy but elegant, if not attractive (for this is not always possible at such an age!) then with the iconography of attractiveness, a.k.a. style, democratic in that it is available not only to the inherently blessed or wealthy but all that know what to know. It might only be a haircut, or a make of eyeglass, or a particular kind of sneaker.

He heads to Soho, not for art but Euro-trash. There is a store with a line of shirts, exactly the same distance apart, metal hangers separated by little knobs which position them precisely as sculpture. The shirts are pure white but the collars are asymmetrical, one sleeve half-attached, buttons the collar buttonhole cannot fit into. To the unknowing this is chaos, to the knowing. . . .

Gaetan asks the price. $160, expensive for a steward. He smiles at the salesman, then raises an eyebrow. "Okay," he says. "I'll try it on."

"Fa-a-b-u-lous," says the salesman, a parody, leaning against the waxed light wood wall of the dressing room.

"It's all right," says Gaetan judiciously, pursing his lips. His eyes narrow (he cannot help it) when he judges himself thus, in the mirror, as a physical object.

"Much better than all right."

"All right." Gaetan parts his lips, revealing even teeth somewhat yellow because of the cigarettes. The salesman (24, taking classes at Parsons, who lately has been applying cortisone cream to cure a persistent skin problem) does not part his lips, but turns them up at the corner, revealing not amusement but recognition of the attempt, a hierarchical attempt to evince superiority to Gaetan.

Gaetan unbuttons the shirt, pulls the front slowly off revealing his nipples, hardening, in the mirror.

The salesman watches, apparent disinterest. "Would you like it?"

Gaetan flicks his eyes up and down the body in the mirror. "I don't think so, no."

He hands the shirt to the salesman. Without looking at him or the mirror, he slips on his ribbed white undershirt, then buttons his own shirt. He walks past the salesman and stops at the glass counter in the center of the store. There is a watch, of shiny bright chrome, no numerals visible until you move your eye back and forth, when a polarized pattern of the watch face makes them visible. Next to it is one with a shiny black face, faintly smudged. Gaetan asks to look at it. He narrows his eyes as he did with himself in the mirror. The smudges are the black hour and minute hands, black also but matte, each in a stylized shape of one of the two identical initials that form the store's logo.

The salesman explains this, irritating Gaetan, as if he had not discerned this himself. "I'll take it," he interrupts.

"It's two hundred and fifty dollars," the salesman says (good money at the time), as if Gaetan cannot afford it.

Truly annoyed, Gaetan puts the watch on his wrist, takes out a green plastic card.

The salesman checks the number on the card before placing the plastic watch case and Gaetan's old watch in a bag (shiny black with matte black initials imprinted horizontal) identical in style to the watch. This bag, this watch is recognizable by those who know what to know.

"Fabulous," says the first salesman.

"It tells the time," says Gaetan, of that which the watch does not do.

"You're French?"

"*Quebecois.*"

"Oh." The salesman hands him the check to sign, then gives him the card. "I've been to Montreal. I liked it very much. The people were so. . .friendly."

"So they say."

10

Gaetan's hands are tied to the iron sides of the bed. The strokes of leather are not hard enough to evince more than perfunctory cries of "oh. . .stop. . ." but he cries out "for real" when the fourth finger, and the thumb, enter his body. More popper is shoved under his nose, and the lights under his eyes (yellow orange on dark brown) spread outward in pools of glowing orange, like the sun and its shooting corona up close, burns but interesting. He bucks his legs purposelessly, an insect. It is dark and he cannot see what is shoved in his mouth but it smells like an old sock. More poppers. Although outraged, his body, in a sense, responds.

Later they leave him. He sleeps, wakes enraged. He stalks through the halls looking for the men, but it's hopeless, only a glimpse as they entered the darkened room. "Is something wrong?" the attendant asks. Gaetan goes to the shower room. Here, at least, it is bright. He stands with his eyes shut under the water, eyes closed but face up-tilted, a memory of exploding orange circles, oblivious to those watching him. When someone tries to play he swats the hand away. Outside the club he realizes the watch, not waterproof, has stopped. He means to repair it but forgets. By the time he returns to New York he has accepted it as an icon, a symbol that he knows what to know, wears it as a bracelet. Anyone he meets after this (over the age of 35, that is) must give some indication of being aware of this.

On a beach in Cartagena he sticks it in his sandal. When he returns from the water, it is gone.

11

His childhood is uninteresting. He never discusses it. He had a mother, a father, a brother who is an accountant but wanted to race cars. Gaetan wanted to be in the movies, or at least be in the movie magazines. When he is 16 he meets a man who promises to do a portfolio of him so he can become a model. But before the man can shoot him in clothing he must photograph him naked, so that he can analyze as how to best drape the clothes over his body. Years later, in a porn shop, Gaetan stops, returns to the earlier page. Yes, he is pretty sure, that is him, legs up past his ears, his smallish member protruding straight up, invisible pillows propping up the then-awkward position.

He buys the magazine with the idea of masturbating to it, the memory of his younger self. But the thin, almost hairless body disturbs him, reminds his nervous system if not his mind of something. He stops, cannot sleep, gets up and goes down to the street. He pretends it is to buy a pack of cigarettes, but that is not the reason. The reason?

12

The clouds obscure the engine with cotton balls, the kind Tom used to take his make-up off after his act at Club 82. "You've got to admit, I'm a beautiful girl," Tom liked to say. Tom was a beautiful girl but a remarkably plain boy and as many times as he had seen it he could never connect the two together. If he loved anybody he loved Tom but more likely he didn't love anybody.

The engines drone. The lights are down. The passengers sleep. In the back, near the bathrooms, he chats with a guy in a polo shirt and jeans, one of those three-day beards. Dave is in music promotion. He refused all meals and drank only hot water which he flavored with wedges of lemon. He had read this was the way to avoid jet lag. "But I've seen you somewhere," says Dave.

Gaetan, handsome, memorable, shrugs.

"Do you know where Fire Island is?" Dave asks.

Gaetan nods. "Yes, but I've never been there."

"Perhaps you'd like to visit sometime?"

"Yes."

13

He orders *boudin blanc*, Jean-Paul skirt steak. The room is noisy and hot, cigarette smell on their clothing. They are discussing boyfriends, sex, movies, soccer, the state of their health. Both are having trouble sleeping, and as a consequence are tired all the time. That's the trouble with coke, damned if you do or don't take sleeping pills. They discuss the feasibility of stopping or at least cutting down on the use of this drug.

"We're getting old," says Jean-Paul.

"I'm not even 30!" exclaims Gaetan.

"You're 32," says Jean-Paul.

"I'm 29," says Gaetan. He shows a skeptical Jean-Paul his driver's license. Yes, the birthdate is 1952. It really is peculiar because they went to school together, and Jean-Paul and Gaetan both have believed, until this moment, they were in the same form. Jean-Paul quit earlier, of course, but that was for the Army.

They order coffee. "Let's walk," suggests Jean-Paul. So they do, to the river, but instead of going into the bar they cross the street. "Here, doggie," calls Gaetan, but the dog retreats from the bench. The water slaps against the piling, slap, slap, slap. Gaetan closes his eyes. He wakes up startled, heart racing. "Jean-Paul," he calls.

Panicked, he looks for Jean-Paul. Yes, that's his black leather jacket. As he approaches, Jean-Paul turns, zipping up his pants. Gaetan stops. Is that a body at his feet? "No," says Jean-Paul. "I—" He was only pissing. It is not a body, but a piece of wood and its shadow, magnifying it. Jean-Paul wraps the jacket around him. "It's freezing," Gaetan says (though it's not). But his hair is wet with sweat.

Bad as he feels, it does not stop him from getting up early the next morning to take the train to the ferry.

I Flunked
Masturbation Class

Some women come easy, some come hard, and some don't come at all. In my search for the Excalibur of sensation, I had tried everything from consciousness-raising to Jungian analysis to an improvised version of Musical People more suitable to the road company of "Let My People Come" than a Jewish dropout from the Ivy League. So it was with a feeling both of anticipation and deja vu that I looked forward to meeting Betty Dodson, who is to female eroticism what Bobby Orr is to puck chasing. An artist friend of mine had encountered her in Berkeley—where Betty lives when she's not in New York— and had spoken about her in terms usually reserved for descriptions of the Second Coming. I decided I would be content with the first.

Beauty is in the eye of the beholder. The forty-two-year-old sexual guru of the Women's Movement sports a crewcut both above and below the waist. Ten years ago she was making erotic paintings by day and going to A.A. meetings at night. She started doing yoga in 1969, and in 1972 held her first workshops, In them, she teaches other women how to get along better with their bodies—in particular, to have better and bigger orgasms. Betty has sex with men, women, and vibrators. But she always sleeps alone,

I took a taxi to Betty's apartment. A nude six-year-old girl—the daughter of Barbara, a neighbor who assists Betty in running the workshops—answered the door. She told me to leave my coat and shoes in the hall and go into the bedroom to undress. I felt odd as I walked through the living room, for on the deep brown wall-to-wall carpeting sat fourteen naked women, my classmates. They were mainly suburban house-wives in their thirties and forties. At twenty-seven I was clearly the youngest. Most of them sat hunched over, arms around drawn-up knees, embarrassed at the nudity that revealed stretch marks, moles, sagging breasts, Caesarean sec-tion scars. They were surrounded by the accoutrements of slick American sex—stereo speaker, large pillows, bowls of fruit, handcrafted pottery mugs of herbal tea.

I slowly got undressed in the bedroom where a second set of speakers was softly playing Elton John. By the time I got myself some mint tea, the session was ready to begin and the little girl who had answered the door was sent—fully clothed and protesting—to her apartment down the hall.

It was not difficult to pick out Betty from this circle of overfed and under-exercised women. Her muscular body, glis-tening with coconut oil, is a walking advertisement for her workshop. Which is lucky for her. Although she still sells prints and drawings, she now makes her living almost exclu-sively from workshops, lectures (at colleges, women's groups, and psychological associations), and writings (she has just finished a book on masturbation).

The first order of business was for us to introduce our-selves and explain why we had come to this sexual workshop.

Molly was the first to speak:

"I can't masturbate to climax in front of anybody but my husband," she said.

"You think *that's* bad," said Margaret. "I can only come by myself!"

"Did you ever try using a vibrator with another human being?" asked Betty.

"Yes," said Margaret, shrugging her shoulders. "But it doesn't help. I just get embarrassed."

"My husband and I have an open marriage," confided Elsa. 'During this last year I got very involved with a woman. I was in love with her. Since then the relationship has broken up but I think I'm basically gay. I'd like to explore that aspect of myself a little more. Especially because I find it harder to get an orgasm with a woman than a man."

"That's probably because you're not as used to it," suggested Betty.

"I don't have trouble getting orgasms, either with other people or by myself," said Flossie. "But I'd like to get more of them—and whenever I want to!"

What these women were looking for—and finding—was an affirmation of their generally unconventional lifestyles. They had good lives they wanted to make better. Many of them were swingers. They got it on alone and in groups. With their husbands, friends, lovers, and vibrators. At swingers' clubs and parties and weekends. They had houses in the country and love pads in the city. There were women whose husbands took separate vacations, and women whose daily lives seemed *la dolce vita* in Isla Mujeres. Many of them had platonic but apparently happy marriages with men who over the years had turned into "best friends." They had children and money (a workshop of four sessions costs sixty dollars). None of them seemed to share my particular problem.

Oddly enough, I was the only woman from the city.

"I think that a lot of the so-called feminists—single women, professional women—don't feel they need help, or that they have other things to occupy themselves," explained Betty. "It's the suburban housewife who knows she wants to make changes."

One of the changes Betty suggested we make had to do with keeping ourselves in shape. "Women systematically mistreat their bodies," she said, flinging around a set of five-pound barbells. "We're conditioned not to develop our arm and leg muscles—because it's considered *masculine* to be strong. We wear bras and girdles that hinder our natural movements. We never exercise our pelvic muscles—even though they're essential to carrying a baby." Exercising the pelvic muscles is not one of Betty's problems. She can twist her genitalia with the agility of Gypsy Rose Lee.

We spent the rest of the first session doing maneuvers that were a combination of yoga and the Royal Canadian Air Force exercise book. As we squatted and stretched and breathed and lifted, Betty individually fixed our postures in front of the floor-to-ceiling mirror that covers one wall of her living room. According to her diagnosis, I would have been 4-F from the Girl Scouts.

Before we left we got our first homework assignment: to masturbate a minimum of one hour a day, preferably with a vibrator.

If the vibrator is to the women's movement as the Pill was to the sexual revolution, Betty deserves a sales commission for her tireless promotion of Japan's kinkiest nonhuman export. . .the Panasonic Panabrator: a large, heavy, disc-headed, variable-speed pleasure machine that is the Harley Chopper of technological turners-on. But the electric-powered Panabrator can only be used in relative proximity to a wall socket. So there is no danger that the handheld, penis-shaped cheapies will go the way of the Edsel or the pinhole camera.

"What I hate most about camping trips," complained Betty, "is that I'm stuck with my portable!"

"All those batteries. . ." commiserated Barbara.

"The very first thing I do when I get home," continued Betty, "even before opening my mail or checking the telephone service, is run to my Panabrator!"

The advantages of the Panabrator over a hand are these: (1) it never tires, and (2) you do not have to cut its fingernails.

The disadvantages, other than its lack of portability, are these: (1) a persistent drone (reminiscent of an electric razor); (2) an increased electrical bill; (3) its tendency to irritate the pubic region; and (4) a dehumanization that in extreme instances can result in one's inability to have orgasm with a human being.

The latter problem doesn't bother Betty much because she does not depend on her partner to climax. She says she's been able to do that herself since she was five. She does not strive for simultaneous orgasm. Her emphasis is on self-love, both sexually and physically.

"Look in the mirror and talk to yourself. Tell yourself you're beautiful, you're wonderful. Women are so involved with the romantic image of themselves that by themselves, they think they're nothing. Learn to be relaxed and loving with yourself first, *then* with someone else. Self-loathing is a longstanding habit that we can break! "

Betty joyously exhibited her favorite masturbation position: back on the floor, head on a pillow against the wall, knees up and apart.

We faithfully experimented with her various sized and shaped gizmos, careful to place a towel between our labia and the vibrating heads—lest our genitalia swell to the gigantic proportions of the penis-sized clitoris of the Kikuyus, a Kenyan tribe in which the females spend a large part of their adolescence yanking on their vulvae.

The next week we compared notes.

Chris had bought a Panabrator and loved it.

"I laughed and laughed when I came," she said. "It was terrific!"

"Did you try using it with someone else?" asked Betty.

"Not yet, but I will!"

June did not have such a positive experience. "I prefer using my hand," she admitted. "I got off so quickly it wasn't any fun."

"Oh, that's no good!" exclaimed Betty. "I could come in two minutes if I wanted to. But now I won't even bother unless I have at least half an hour to play with myself. Did you fantasize?" she asked.

June shrugged: "It wasn't necessary."

"But it's important," said Betty. "Women have to start creating their own sexual imagery, instead of using the media images of Hollywood, or TV, or advertising. Caress yourself. Love yourself. The last thing you should do is concentrate on the orgasm."

Later in the session we tape-recorded our fantasies. The pillaging Russian army. Interspecies loving. Rows of men dangling in harnesses like hunks of slaughtered meat in a Chicago packing house. S&M. B&D. Water sports. Everyone had their special favorites that—like the U.S. post office—would make them come despite wind, rain, and flaccid dicks.

"I'm worried about this rape fantasy I have," questioned Roberta. "It seems so anti-feminist. But it always gets me off."

Betty turned to her. "Try something else," she suggested. "Like a loving C-R session that turns into an orgy. Stay with it a while. Then, if it doesn't work, you can always go back to your six brutal Irish cops!"

"Have you ever tried to live out a fantasy?" asked Margaret.

"Sure!" said Betty. "It can be liberating, but it can also destroy the fantasy. I used to masturbate pretending I was fucking a German shepherd. Finally I did it. It was exciting, but after that the fantasy just didn't get me off. So I switched to something else!"

Talking about fantasies made us revert to playing with the vibrators. But no amount of technological assistance had solved my problem. Out of pity for my lonesome plight, the group decided to masturbate precisely at midnight the following evening as psychic support.

The results of that night will remain a secret between me, the group, and the wonderful folks who brought us Pearl Harbor.

We began the third session by giving each other body massages á la Esalen—lots of coconut oil and continuous arm rotation. After becoming sufficiently relaxed, or excited, we then proceeded to look into our bodies the way gynecologists do. For many "students" this was the high point of the workshop experience.

"Mind-blowing!" said June.

"A whole new world!" said Molly. Next we tried out the perineometer, a device doctors use to measure the strength of vaginal contractions. Survivors of multiple episiotomies use it to strengthen the walls of the uterus to prevent prolapses. My classmates and I tested our sexual prowess with it.

It was no surprise that I came in last. I peaked at 35, whereas the mean for our group was around 50. Huffing and puffing, Betty passed 100—clear off the charts—to our muted cheers. I vowed that next week I would devote more time to my homework.

The last session was the one everybody had been waiting for. Classmates who had skipped the second or third session— all were there. For this was the week of the sexual demonstrations. (Due to legal considerations, Betty has since discontinued this aspect of the workshop.)

Betty's first partner was Doug Johns—a male artist who makes casts of vulvae. Often when he makes the casts he also makes his models. And, according to Melody, he is an excellent, thoughtful, tender lover.

But this night he was a washout. He had the chic male failing—impotence. Despite all that Betty—and later Molly and Brenda and Margot—could do, he couldn't keep it up. But it did not deter the determined women of the group, about a third of whom were soon working on Doug and/or each other. The rest of us sat around munching fruit, playing with the vibrators, and looking at our more active classmates pleasuring each other.

Finally Doug left—sans orgasm, but with our good vibes, for he had maintained grace under what could be considered most trying circumstances.

"It was *interesting* that he couldn't get it up," said June.

We all agreed he was a good sport, if not exactly the guy you'd choose to spend a furlough from the Women's House of Detention with.

We anxiously awaited the arrival of Eleanor—Betty's friend, our classmate, and the woman whom Betty had chosen to do her lesbian demonstration with.

"Sorry I'm late," she said, as she breezed in around 9:30, "but I spent all day at home practicing with a friend!" She got undressed in a flash and then climbed on top of Betty—after carefully placing a Panabrator between their genitalia. They lay, face-to-face, very businesslike, as the vibrator hummed. It was about as sexy as watching Telly Savalas brush his teeth. After a while they came, or at least they stopped. I don't know. I was eating an apple and watching somebody else chew gum.

Sally said she thought it was a peculiar way to demonstrate homosexual loving—especially for those of us who had never experimented with bisexuality. "I mean," she exclaimed, "I still wouldn't know what to *do!*"

I went into the bedroom to put on my blue jeans. Most of the group was still sprawling casually, drinking mint tea, and discussing the implications of the evening. As I left, Betty was illustrating another of her favorite masturbation positions: heels pressed together, lotus-style, feet drawn up close to the body, head resting against a large pillow. Three women sat in a semicircle imitating her.

The sound of the vibrators was like the drone of a lawn mower on a hot summer evening. It's a pleasant sound, if you like lawn mowers.

Heel

One day, after I had arrived and undressed as was my custom, she asked my permission to place something in my mouth that would prevent me from speaking. Naturally I agreed. After placing a dirty sock in my mouth, she said: "Our relationship has become tedious to me. I am tired of your complaints, your groveling, even your protestations of love. It is all so predictable—the commands and disobediences, apologies and the punishments, the wielding of the rod and shaft. Perhaps you have suspected this, or have become bored yourself—" Unable (as always, due to the blindfold) to signal with my eyes, or now even to respond verbally, I shook my head exaggeratedly, like a bad theatrical actress, at these suggestions—for I had never been less bored in my life, nor had it occurred to me that she might be. "I must believe you, but frankly, I am surprised—you who have always professed such intelligence and curiosity, such boredom with routine, to be so content with the standard cliches. But in any case, regardless of your personal feelings, surely a person with your great powers of understanding—or so you have always told me—will be able to comprehend and even empathize if I tell you of my unhappiness?" Though indeed I had neither understanding nor empathy, I had no choice but to nod an affirmative. "Good. Then I hope you will not object to a slight change in the ground rules of our contract. It is a small one, but of course you must agree to it. . ." She paused, and I wondered what it could be—branding of the torso? public display of my face? removal of the blindfold?—and whether I would be able to resist it, should that seem prudent, even if I wished to. She asked if I were curious to hear what it was, or would I rather simply end our relationship then and there? Naturally I shook my head at this latter suggestion and she stated her request, which seemed so insignificant that I was somewhat disappointed (as well as relieved) to hear that it would involve wearing a device (she specifically avoided the word "gag") that would prevent me from speaking. On occasion she might remove this object, but the slightest word from my lips would suffice to return it.

"One implication you should consider," she said, "is that the safe words will no longer be in effect. I should hope that by this point you have gained a degree of trust both in my actions and perceptions, so that I would be able to anticipate if you are in imminent danger, but I might as well inform you, so that you may make your decision with as much knowledge and little anxiety as possible, that the infliction of bodily pain will no longer be a prime component of our relationship. As you can imagine, it is tiresome in the extreme to have to recapitulate the earlier phases of the pain progression before new intensities of anguish are achieved—this in spite of the fact that the progression is itself being continually foreshortened (for periods of transition, unlike those of stasis, are unable to be replicated—surely you know this from your studies of operant conditioning in rodents, long ago in college, about which you once insisted—at great and somewhat tedious length!—on informing me). It has also become clear to me that—due to the combination of pride, stubbornness, and perversity in your character, that in your wholehearted embracing of what so far has been relatively mild punishments—there is simply no degree of pain, no ritual of endurance, you would not be unwilling to undergo, if only to demonstrate (as if anyone were interested!) that of all human beings, you are the one able to tolerate the most degree of pain. Yes, you'd be willing to prove this even unto death, wouldn't you?" And her hands went around my neck, and I melted into her thumbs until I almost blacked out, when she laughed and let go.

"But though you desire it, or half-desire it, I will not allow you to trick me into using your body like a pin-cushion" (little pinpricks as she said this) "or as a carcass to be carved" (yes, I felt a knife), "or a sewer into which all the world may rid itself of its bodily excrescences. I refuse to thrill your vanity by such ostentatious displays. But I am willing to assign a new role and tasks to you, provided I have your acquiescence." Then she spelled out in some detail what would be required of me.

I was, of course, distressed and confused, and when she took off my gag to allow me to address her for the final time I told her such, but she was adamant: either I acquiesced immediately, without demurral, to what was required, or I would be banished from her presence forever. Although her desires neither interested nor intrigued me they seemed to entail no obvious danger, so I assented—but I cannot pretend I would not have done so anyway, no matter what had been required. And so, after protestations of love that she had little patience for, and suggestions of alternative practices to which she paid no attention, I found myself agreeing to all her conditions. Immediately after this my new life began.

I was to live it on my hands and knees, with a leash on a collar around my neck. A chain was placed linking my arms, and also between my legs, so that I could separate my limbs only the width of my body; a leather mechanism held my tongue in a manner that prevented me from speaking in a comprehensible fashion, although I would be able to mouth barks, woofs, yelps, and other canine vocalizations. Thus muted and accoutered, she began to teach me the proper mode of accompanying her ("sitting," "kneeling," "staying," & so forth—not just in accordance to voice commands, but in response to movements of the leash) as well as certain canine tricks such as shaking hands, rising on my hind legs for a cracker, etc. Once I had mastered these movements, she summoned Charlie, and she trained the two of us to walk together, side-by-side, without nipping or jostling.

Much came relatively easily, but I had trouble making convincing dog sounds. My growl was deemed adequate, but my barks, yelps, bow-wows, and yips were not.

She ordered Charlie to demonstrate, and I was forced to imitate him until my voice grew hoarse. Despite our bizarre duet, my sounds remained hopelessly human, and with but a lone and absentminded caress of the leash (a sad contrast to the whipping of yore) I was ordered to lie in a corner until I demonstrated that I was ready to be "a good dog."

She turned her attentions to Charlie. I could hear the thumping of his tail on the floor and the yelps of happiness as they played. Hungry, thirsty, and (I admit) jealous, I began whimpering.

For a second I wondered from whence the sound had come, it sounded so much like a dog's.

"*Good* dog." She patted the ground and made a smacking sound with her lips. I had often heard her use this signal as a way of summoning Charlie, so I left my corner and padded over to her.

"*Very* good," she exclaimed when I came, petting me excessively, exaggerating the rise and fall of the pitch of her voice as if she were talking to a child. "Perhaps you may end up becoming a good pet after all." She stroked my nose, and scratched behind my ears, and I have to admit it was very soothing. She then ordered me to lie on my back so my tummy was exposed and, my paws in the air (the chain prevented me from letting them fall to my side), she tickled my stomach. I had the same impulse to roll around and snort as the dogs I have tickled there have done.

"Don't hold back. Be what you are," she said. Next to me, Charlie snorted and thumped his tail, then he must have gotten up, because I felt his warm breath over me. I turned my head away, but she ordered me to remain still as he licked my nose and eyelids. Even when he stopped, his mouth must have remained open, for I felt a few drops of saliva land on my lips. I began to retch.

"Lick him back," she ordered.

Time slowed, stopped. When it picked up again, I extended, with great reluctance, my tongue. Luckily it was a part of my body in which Charlie had only minimal interest, for he barely touched it with his own. I was torn between immediately pulling my tongue back in my mouth, so he could not lick any more, or keeping it extended, so his saliva would evaporate off before I put it back in my mouth.

I heard an electric can opener puncturing a can, and the whine of the can as the blade cut into the rotating aluminum, and the sound of a spoon knocking against the side of a dish. She placed what I could smell was a bowl of dog food in front of me and commanded me to eat it.

I have always been afraid of vomiting. Breathing only through my mouth so I would not smell, I extended my tongue. I felt but did not taste the cold wet of the food. The tip of my nose touched the meat. Can I really do this? I thought. Although not as disturbing as spreading my legs for Charlie, it was somehow more disgusting. To my relief Charlie began to edge me out of the way, but she grabbed him and pushed my head into the bowl. Some of the food entered my mouth and some slid up my nostrils, overwhelming me with its smell and making it difficult to breathe. "Swallow," she said, and she held my nose in the meat until I did.

Then Charlie was allowed to join me. I could feel his cold nose, the tickle of his whiskers, smell his breath, as he quickly and noisily devoured the food. Afterwards he licked me, slobbering bits of wet meat on my face such that, even though he had his fill of the water bowl before I did, I did not mind immersing my face in it, in hopes of washing off food and saliva. But some meat stuck in my nostrils, like little dried up balls of snot.

In the other acts of degradation I had undergone, there had always been the mitigating factor of extreme physical sensation, however painful and perverse. But there was none here—just humiliation and a growing rage. The next time she came near me, I attempted to sink my teeth into her ankle. Although she was wearing boots and I bit leather instead, her fury was indescribable; she leashed me to a post, placed a muzzle over my jaws, then whipped me with a bullwhip until, when I was on the verge of passing out, she stopped and rubbed wintergreen into my wounds. This combination of sensations—torments both concentrated and diffuse, continuous and transitory, penetrating and superficial, of paddle-like dullness and needle-like sharpness—managed to at last evoke in me the proper canine howls; I remember her commenting on this shortly before I lost consciousness. Still in agony when I awoke, but chastened, I drooled over the boots I had tried to sink my teeth into until, after many hours, I was forgiven.

In subsequent sessions, she refined my costume: binding my fingers so that I could not use my hands in the normal fashion, also placing pads under my palms and over my knees. The latter I welcomed as they eased the burden on my joints, but I was less happy when one day I found little claws or nails attached to the pads on my palms and on the soles of my feet, so that when I moved across the floor I clicked like Charlie. A tail, also, was added, hanging from a chain which she placed around my waist. I was unable to manipulate it like a real tail, but I grew to like the weight of it hanging off me, and the tickle of its fur against the soft skin of my ass. As my barks etc. remained erratic she replaced the leather in my mouth with a metal chain that went under my tongue and attached to my collar, which forced my tongue into an angle that improved my vocalizations. It hurt to hold my jaw shut, so I tended to let it drop and began drooling like a dog.

Initially I had been as before—naked or nearly so—but one day, when I was quietly waiting in the pointer position, she presented me with my "coat," which she said was made from the skin of a dead dog. I could not tell if this were so, or whether it was made from some other sort of animal, but its texture and smell were certainly mammalian in nature.

This costume came in several parts: one that slipped on like a pair of tights, but with a huge area cut out exposing my crotch and anus, and another which I pulled over my head, like a sweater cut high and short, so that it covered my arms but stopped above the nipples. The feel of the skin was soft and supple; the hairs long and silky, much finer than Charlie's coarse hairs. Although I could not see its color, from remarks she let drop I somehow gathered it was black.

At first Charlie seemed confused by my costume, sniffing repeatedly as if he did not know who I was, but he soon grew accustomed to and even seemed to like it (often rubbing his body against the furs on my back in a manner I can only describe as sensual); indeed, I liked it myself, rather missing it on those occasions when she preferred to leave me naked. Meanwhile my training continued. I learned to retrieve balls, fetch slippers, balance on my hind legs with a ball on my nose, leap onto furniture, etc. At various times I was confined to a metal cage whose size was scarcely sufficient for me to change position, sometimes in reaction to various behavioral miscues or clumsinesses on my part, and sometimes, I felt, because she was, even in this new role, becoming tired of me. As I invariably fell asleep in this cage, I became increasingly unable to gauge the length of time I spent with her. More than once I emerged from her building to find myself in the light of a new day or even in the twilight of the next. This confusion about time caused me to miss what few remaining appointments I had, and because I could offer no explanation, I virtually ceased to return phone calls, maintaining contact only with Leslie and the occasional cursory e-mail to the current. Soon the memory of my TAD was filled with unanswered messages, at which point it ceased to pick them up entirely.

Outside of the time I had tried to bite her (I never attempted this again, as she assured me that should I do so the muzzle would be placed on me without hope of removal) she abjured punishments of a physical nature, or rather, these were so mild in nature and short in duration that they satisfied none of my physical needs, and served only to inflame memories of times gone by. One time my resentment grew such that I decided not to return. Huddling under my comforter (though the day was indeed warm and I had not turned on the air-conditioner), I waited in trepidation for her call, which came when I was scarcely an hour late for our appointment. Without, of course, allowing me to speak (it had been over a week since she had heard my human voice), she reminded me of the penalties for failing to honor our contract, and catalogued in concise but pungent detail the contents of merely one of the videotapes of myself in her possession. Before hanging up, as a kind of *coup de grace*, she addressed me by my real first name—a lucky guess, perhaps, but perhaps not. What if she had had me followed, or had my fingerprints traced, and could humiliate me before all the world? Realizing how utterly lost I was, I apologized profusely and immediately made my way to her. From then on I ceased even token resistance to her future requests, no matter how disgusting or bizarre.

As it turned out, however, to my surprise and delight, this further degree of renunciation precipitated the re-emergence of my eroticism. True, what excitements I experienced derived almost solely from a mental and emotional appreciation of my degradation rather than from a physical stimulus, but this became so deeply gratifying, for reasons it seemed useless to explore with a shrink, that I ceased mourning simpler pleasures; it also left me free to revert to what I suppose was my 'animal nature,' so that when in fact I was finally ordered to have intercourse with Charlie, the pleasure allowed myself, paradoxically, was no longer merely conceptual, as it had been in that long-off time (scarcely two months ago) when I had agreed to our contract, but physical, for I had learned to appreciate that Charlie and I were both sentient beings who, from other sides of the species and language divide, were able to partake of shared sensations.

When I hinted at such to my friend Leslie, her stomach turned in disgust, but was it really so different from being turned on by a human being of another nationality and language, such as occurred between John Smith and Pocahontas, or the *Bounty* mutineers when they landed on Tahiti? I think not.

Charlie's penis was not large, of course, compared to a human's, and, by ejaculating almost instantaneously, he made no attempt to prolong my pleasure; on the other hand, having been ordered by my owner to imitate as closely as possible the physiogonomy as well as the behavior of a *bitch*, I contracted my vagina around his organ to prevent its withdrawal, not releasing it until perhaps half an hour had passed; his struggles to disentangle himself during this period caused her great satisfaction, albeit unintentional on *his* part. My hair was soaked with perspiration, as were my knees that held the weight of my body, and my back and ass as well (though this was perhaps due to sweat and other bodily fluids), a slippery surface Charlie and I continually forced ourselves against. My owner kindly cradled my head in her arms as Charlie made his attempts to rid himself of me, complimenting me upon the degrees to which I would go to prove myself worthy of her attentions, and the empathy and "fraternity" (in the French sense of the word) with which I was able to commune with a member of another species.

"You are a true canine," she said, as she petted me, and I was grateful for the remark, as, after such a strenuous evening, I was grateful for the canned food with which she rewarded our acrobatics, and of which, after all (according to the newspapers) a portion of our elderly routinely partake.

On the way home I usually purchased a Haagen Daz ice cream bar, partly because the canned and dry dog food (albeit nutritious) only stimulated my craving for sugar, and partly to erase the residue of meaty flavor from my mouth.

I stared at myself in the mirror after one such occasion. To my surprise it was scarcely past midnight when I had left her building (I felt sure it would be the following afternoon), the streets full of revelers, with whom I felt an incredible camaraderie, as if, not subject to her proscriptions, I could go home with any or all and happily perform whatever acts came into our heads. Indeed, as I walked past female couples in the East Village, I began to wonder how it would be to command them to perform such acts together with an animal I should myself acquire—more out of artistic curiosity than any specifically *sexual* desire—to be on the other side of the looking glass, as it were. Such knowledge is always useful for a writer. I wondered how much money this would entail, since I had neither the time or inclination to commence a relationship similar in structure (but opposite in role) to the one I was already in.

Thinking such thoughts, and picturing various breeds, I felt extraordinarily awake and light on my feet, experimenting landing first on my heel, then on the ball, then my toe, as if I had taken just the right amount of cocaine and would be able to stay up, with the same degree of curiosity and alertness, for days.

My face in the mirror was light and bright. My degrada-tion had brought me through the dark tunnel and out the other side, so that, contrary to habit, I lay in bed without washing or brushing my teeth, my arms spread wide, as if to welcome whatever phantoms would come in the night.

One day I found my costume altered—or, rather, *enlarged*—so that my ass, genitals, and nipples were also cov-ered in skin. I began to sweat, and the heat and moistness brought out the odors of the skin, making me rather nau-seous. "Hot, isn't it?" my owner asked. I yelped my assent, and drank contentedly out of the bowl that I had so recently scorned. "Nice night for a walk, don't you think? You're well-trained enough, aren't you, not to embarrass your owner in public?" And I heard the metal clank as she picked up the leash.

I began barking furiously—not because I did not consid-er myself sufficiently trained, but because of what she had said about appearing in public. The various amendments of our contract had never even mentioned any abrogation of my right to privacy. I ran away, to a little area under her bed from which she always had difficulty extracting me; when she reached under with her hand to drag me out, I grabbed her wrist in my mouth. It was less a bite than a grab, but when she tried to resist I dug my teeth in deeper, so that I felt the skin tear and for the first time I tasted the heady, salty taste of human blood. This unleashed a surprisingly intense desire to crunch my teeth through her bones, one that had less to do with my anger at her than a kind of primeval impulse towards the consummation of raw flesh. But knowing full well the dangers of a human bite, I hovered, paralyzed.

She herself had also stopped moving, as if refusing to dignify this struggle. Eventually, without even a word, I released her.

To my surprise she did not attempt to punish me, even to remind me of her previous threat, but merely spoke. "The agreement was not that you would not *appear* in public, but that your identity would be concealed. Dressed as you will be, no one could possibly recognize you, and there will be additional pads under your palms and on your knees so that you will not unduly pressure or scrape yourself.

"You will, of course, be on the leash, and will walk by my side, obeying my commands. You will hold yourself erect, your back straight, your head raised and alert. You will smell tires and trees and the street as I direct you, and will in all manners act as I have taught. People may try to pet you; if so, let them. Do not bite. If other dogs approach, you will let them sniff and play with you, unless of course I command you not to.

"At a certain point you may find you need to relieve yourself. You will tug three sharp times on your leash to inform me of this, at which time I will place a newspaper under you and you will do your business. This may happen more than once, perhaps many times.

"What we are demonstrating, although you may not understand it as such, is evidence of the trust between you and me." At this point she took my head in her hands. "Public display is not something that could have been done in the beginning of our relationship; indeed, I have never reached such a stage with a dog so quickly, especially one with so little prior training. Perhaps if there had been no time limit. . ." she mused. "In any case, as you have put your trust in me, I put mine in you. It is not inconceivable that some figure of authority may approach to question us. If such occurs, you will of course allow me to reply. Only if directly addressed by such a figure will you speak, and you will answer as I shall: that we are rehearsing a scene for a movie, called *The Secret Life of Canines*, in which humans play the part of dogs.

"If in this or any other matter you disobey me, your leash and collar and costume will immediately be removed, and you will become a stray, with no keys, no clothing, no money, no identification. . .in addition, of course, to the other consequences of breaking your contract. Is this understood?" I barked a "yes," in the way she had taught me to signify yes, but then began to thump my feet in protest.

"I see you find the idea of a public appearance distressing. Your wishes have no consequence, and of course you will do as I order." She ordered me into the kitchen, where I shared a plate of what had the taste and consistency of a rather coarse version of country pate with Charlie. Then I was ordered to drink from a special bowl which Charlie was forbidden to share. The liquid had a thick and somewhat medicinal cherry taste, which was nonetheless not unpleasant, though it contrasted a bit oddly with the pate.

"You have just swallowed a laxative," she informed me. "It should take effect within half an hour. Despite your evident fears, I have a strong suspicion you will be happy to relieve yourself, even in public. We will commence our descent to the street now, and you will show me how well you have learned your lessons."

She had given me enemas and laxatives before, but the prospect of going to the bathroom before strangers was so humiliating that besides this the fear of merely being *observed* by strangers paled.

Before we left she had me sit on my haunches, and very carefully placed a large and heavy helmet, or mask, over my head. It had considerable weight, and made breathing difficult, even if you ignored its extremely unpleasant odor—a sickly sweet combo of animal nature and formaldehyde. I gathered its nose was pointy, for I subsequently found myself banging it, more than once, into a wall. Nonetheless, I wore it gladly, sure it would serve its intended function, which was to conceal my identity from those who would shortly be seeing me.

Few of you, perhaps, have ever tried to descend several flights of stairs solely on your hands and knees. It is difficult, stressful, and extremely slow work. Each new placing of a limb shocks by the coldness of the stone step, then the pressure of the stone against one's knees (quickly turning to pain), ever accompanied by the fear of sliding. I started, as humans do, headfirst, but gravity and momentum almost caused me to go into a somersault; I had to push against a lowered step with all my arm strength to prevent this from happening, and then my legs slid from under me down the steps so I was more or less akimbo, stomach hugging the steps, arms clutching above as if I were hanging off a mountain side. I crawled back up till I reached a spot where I could turn side-wise, and I gingerly rearranged myself on the step, so that I could lower one leg over the edge horizontally, and then bring the other to meet it, much as I had, on more than one occasion, sidestepped down a steep ski slope. This was a cumbersome process not without its own dangers, as two legs could barely fit together on one step. In addition, my crotch became severely stretched, both horizontally and vertically, in this attempt to move from higher step to lower. The difficulty and the pain, however, did serve to distract me from contemplation of my public initiation.

The downstairs door opened and I heard the voices of people laughing on the stairs. Their feet made a peculiar echo I didn't recall hearing before, perhaps due to my proximity to the stone through which the sound was carried, a much better medium of transmission than air. They must have entered an apartment on the floor beneath, however, as the sounds of their walking and talking abruptly ceased.

Then a door above us opened and shut, and footsteps descended.

"Another movie?" a man's voice asked, with a hint of irony.

"Yes," said my master. "What do you think of my new 'leading lady'?"

"'Led' lady," you mean," he said. "Very fine. A kind of shepherd, I think, with perhaps a bit of retriever."

"Husky too, she's got a bit of the wolf in her." They continued in this vein for awhile, then I was commanded to shake the man's hand, which I did, balancing myself carefully as I extended a paw.

"Good dog," they both said, petting me in approbation. My owner asked if there was something in his garbage I would enjoy eating.

"I had a lovely steak for dinner yesterday," he said. The bag was opened and I was forced to sniff through it for the bone, which I presented to my master, who commanded me to carry it to the street. I also came up with an empty cookie container, probably Pepperidge Farm, as I could taste the silvery texture with my tongue. Gradually they lost interest in me and began discussing someone called Chip. My owner apparently knew Chip, but did not like him. Other names got mentioned too, some of which clearly belonged to people, some of which I wasn't sure.

After awhile, tiring of our slow pace, the neighbor said good night and headed down the stairs.

Many more minutes passed before my owner and I finally reached the bottom of the stairs.

The air felt refreshing, even with the smell of automobile exhaust and a kind of perfume from flowers or a tree, a name I have heard often but am unable to remember. Honeysuckle? Magnolia? Hyacinth?

The brown stone of the exterior steps was softer and warmer than the marble, and far less slippery. In exhaustion, I collapsed on it. It was wonderful to finally remove the pressure from my hands and knees; the warmth of the stone somewhat helped calm my stomach, which was churning somewhat unpleasantly, from the bone which I still held in my mouth, the laxative, and the exertion.

In short order I was jerked upright, and we descended the final steps to the pavement. Little bits of raised stone it dug through the pads on my hand and knees to prick me, almost as if a pattern were being engraved on my skin. I had played handball and other games on similar sidewalks in my childhood, often returning upstairs with crisscross patterns embedded on my knees and legs. It was a pleasant memory.

"Heel," she commanded, as I dragged behind her. Due to fatigue and stomach distress, I could barely move. I bumped into something. Metal. Smooth. Then a softer substance, that smelled like tar, but also arugula. A tire. The tire was warmish and soft; through the arugula smell I could detect the rubber beneath.

A second tire (a hint of excrement this time), then I was ordered from the pavement into the street. I tried to resist (this public humiliation somewhat resuscitating my will power) but the leash cut into my collar and I was forced to crawl into the gutter. Tears poured from my eyes, which of course no one could see.

The tar was softer still against my knees, and I enjoyed its smoothness and warmth. Eventually, having recognized that I had become "dirty," that I had been irrevocably tainted by the street, that I was in no sense the person I had been, I ceased my resistance and began to sniff the tires of other cars almost with curiosity, not resisting even when she ordered me to lower my face to some disgusting mess on the street. I worried, of course, about contamination by dogshit, but then recalled that in some sense I *was* a dog, and if I wasn't a dog I was another kind of animal, an animal whose bite was more dangerous than a dog's and therefore maybe my shit was too—so perhaps after all it was *I* who was the menace to civilization, and not the other way around.

I soon found it necessary to tug three times on my leash. Fire was going through my insides, liquid began to leak out. She quickly unhooked some segment of my costume, for I could suddenly feel the moist and slightly coolish night air upon my ass, and, after a newspaper was positioned under me, I indeed found myself with my legs spread apart, glad, as she had predicted, to relieve myself even in public. Feces exited my body in hot, noisy spurts, with a strong but not totally repugnant meat-like smell. A vision of a night in Morocco, when I had squatted, feverish and ill, over a hole in the floor, filled my mind. There had been newspapers there, also, instead of toilet paper, and by dawn I was so exhausted that I had fallen asleep, right there, on that hideous tile floor. Surely this was no worse than that. At first I made every attempt to prevent my emanations from landing on my costume, but when the cramps washed over me I would forget everything save emptying myself. I felt ill and feverish, and lay with my head against her knee, for by now she was squatting next to me, scratching behind my ears and telling me what a good dog I was and how proud, how very proud, she was of me.

I could hear people passing by. It did not seem possible they did not notice anything unusual, but I heard nothing pertaining to me or my situation.

After such humilation, going to the park seemed less punishment than a treat. Indeed, the soft dirt of the dog run was comforting. Strange canines ran up to sniff and mount me, but my owner managed to pull me away before any such encounters could be consummated. It was a pleasure to roll on the grass, now that the gutter had burned the fear of dirt and feces out of me. A number of disparaging references were made as to my appearance, but as no one was in the park at that hour save alkies and drug addicts and the homeless, I did not let these bother me. Indeed, I felt superior, protected;. I had a home, someone who loved me, I was clothed, housed, and fed. Could every being in the park—whether canine or human—say as much?

Upstairs, after a climb that was much easier than the one down, she held my hand as I squatted in the tub and expelled the remaining foods and liquids from my system, then she bathed me in warm soapy water, all the while telling me what a good pet I was, how well I had undertaken my training, how pleased she was that we had reached this new level. Several times the tub was emptied and refilled till any remaining smell of shit and garbage was gone. Then, in the empty tub, she tenderly patted me dry and rubbed lotion all over me and put salve on my scrapes and wounds. Too exhausted from the various insults to mind and body to attempt to move, and resistant to her attempts to haul me out, I lay there, almost in an out-of-body state, as she brought a bowl of water and a toothbrush and brushed my teeth for me. She ordered Charlie to keep me company, and all that night we lay together in the tub, our bodies curled around each other for comfort & warmth.

from *Assumption of the Leash*

Cissy

"Some things are tragedies, some are merely heartbreaks," said Yuri, who had been standing nearby with a far-away look on his face. "I will tell you what happened to me one time, when I was younger and unknowing in the ways of love. I had seen a young woman at a party whom I found myself attracted to, but as she was more than fifteen years younger than me, and, finding myself over-conscious of this disparity, I told myself I would not pay attention to her. She was just out of college, trying to make her way in the downtown art scene, and as she chattered with her friends, some of whom were still in school, others of whom had just graduated, the way they talked about 'the world' and 'the art scene,' with its fake cynicism revealing a touchingly concealed naivete, confirmed my earlier decision not to distract her with my old world cynicism. Nonetheless, her eyes caught mine from time to time, and I half-consciously wondered if perhaps it was my very jadedness which attracted her.

"About this jadedness I have two opinions. Almost surely it is justified, the things experience had taught me had been taught me for a reason, what was the point of age if not to confer Wisdom? On the other hand, if, as Heraclitus has shown, each day, each minute, each second is utterly unique and unreduplicable—perhaps, just perhaps, these lessons are in fact false and misleading—rationalizations we cowards use to conceal from ourselves the utter meaninglessness, pointlessness, etcetera of life. That night, due to the youthfulness of the girl and perhaps the soft summer air, I more than half-hoped my 'perhaps' was the correct alternative, even though this would confirm the very uselessness, irrelevancy, even *vanity* of my experience. For in my more altruistic moments, I told myself the relevancy of my life didn't matter—not just in the grand scheme, of course—but perhaps even to myself. Normally I was totally caught up in the frivolousness of my everyday existence—less frivolous, perhaps, than most people's, but still, in the context of the eternal, vain and superficial—but every once in a while the tedium and repetitiveness of all this would astonish me—as it were—afresh, and I would look at myself as I looked at other people, with amazement at my narcissistic egocentrism. What was I, after all, but a leaf? a blade of grass? a bacterium in the sands of time? Could I honestly pretend that my life was significant or interesting—*even* to myself!—I who watched sports on television every chance I got? Obviously not. And if it was not interesting to me, why should it be interesting to other people, even as a subject of conversation, even though the amusing, self-deprecating (if I may say so myself!) mode in which I invariably spoke about it to other people—so that their laugher would absolve, as it were, my ephemera of its more negative connotations—was as far removed from the earnest, self-pitying, replete-with-*significance* demeanor which others brought to any discussion of their lives. . .oh, complete the simile yourself. I hope I am not being hopelessly obscure.

"As I say, I had no desire to intrude this mass of vanity, ambivalency, and indecision into the world of these optimistic and intelligent, if almost assuredly self-deluded, young people. Even their complexions gleamed with the transparency of youth—not healthily rosy, mind you, for these were aesthetes who eschewed such outward signs of success as tennis, golf, or even jogging—but that which comes from untroubled nights of sleep, or, rather, nights troubled by the enjoyable excesses of youth, not to mention the benefits of a decade or so less of exposure to stresses psychological, environmental, and otherwise, as well as the ravages conferred by the usage of drugs, alcohol, and the destructive effect of the by-products of food digestion on cellular structure (by which I mean the release of free radicals during the digestive process, the harmful effects of which are just beginning to be acknowledged, and whose only known antidote—the various forms of anti-oxidants such as vitamins E and C—are only beginning to be extolled by health food enthusiasts).

"Had I talked of anti-oxidants to Cissy—for such, alas!, was her name—surely I would have wearied her. Had I talked of free radicals to Cissy, she might have imagined I was reminiscing about the failed heroes of my youth—Eldridge Cleary, Dr. Timothy Leary, and so forth. Were I not to talk of such things because they revealed my age, I would perforce have to be constrained in her presence—and who can enjoy one who is constrained?

"So I was content to watch her from a distance, in her perky sun dress and absurd, if charming hat, balance a Tom Collins in her hand. Its transparency and clarity—reinforced rather than clouded by the wedge of lime-green lying gently atop the ice—seemed the objective correlative of the hopeful purity of her being—for she had already told me her paintings, albeit representational in the then-current revival of Neo-Expressionism, tended toward the monochromatic and minimal. As for her shoulders. . . !

"On occasion her eye would roam the room. I confess I did not look away from her, but gazed upon her with what I hoped would appear to be a spontaneous and cheerful smile, as if I had caught her gaze on a sudden too. The first time she ignored it, but the second returned it with astonishing radiance, such that it occurred to me that if I had gone across the room to talk to her she would not have greeted my friendly overtures as remiss. But in accordance with my earlier resolution, I remained content in our unarticulated appraisal of each other.

"Meanwhile dusk was giving way to night, and as the violet in the sky faded to a deeper purple the distinct outlines of the figures of those who had gathered in cheerful clusters in the garden of the first-floor apartment of this New York brownstone began to meld with their surroundings in the comforting softness that accompanies the end of day. In the reduced light it was easier to lose sight of Cissy, in the reduced light I was once or twice nervous that she had disappeared altogether. You must understand that I was not in love, I did not feel I could be in love, she was altogether too much present and 'there' to be the kind of person that tended to arouse that emotion in me. Nonetheless I would have liked to go out with her in the more casual way that people of my acquaintance, when they are sufficiently jaded, on occasion do, the objective distraction rather than love. Indeed, my heart was still getting over the throes of a serious, albeit not especially recent, affliction.

"No doubt if I had been sincere in my resolution not to afflict these young beings with my presence I would have left with some friends who were on their way to another party, but as much as I told myself it would be better for these youthful beings were I to remove myself and the potential attractions of my cynicism (for, of course, the move towards destructiveness is always attractive) from them, I continued to dally, forcing conversation with those I was not especially interested in, pretending an interest in the punch bowl and an enthusiasm for the remainder of cold cuts and cheese which I certainly did not possess. Not that I was not hungry, but I had reached that stage in life where the edibles that satisfied such longings needed to attain a further stage of refinement than they had in my youth—contextual elements notwithstanding. That is, whereas I could enjoyably partake of a hot dog at a baseball game or an outdoor barbecue albeit I could not do so at a Nedicks; as for cheese, unless it were of the richest, runniest, most cholesterol-inducing kind, it no longer seemed an adequate companion to sourdough French bread. As for those who can discourse calmly and rationally on the horrors of vegetable pate, I am not one of them.

"Nonetheless, as I say, I dallied and I loitered—perhaps could even be said to 'malinger'—conversing, chewing, and swallowing in a way that attempted to maintain the mild high I had been experiencing without veering over into the excesses either of sentimentality or sobriety. But as you—certainly those within but even those without the somewhat claustrophobic consolations of the twelve-step fraternity—may recall, it is hard to maintain an air of hopeful expectation for an extended length of time, and I began to wonder if it might not be wise to change the venue of the evening entirely. I began, even, to question whether it might be damaging to my dignity to be there, in the midst of so many recent college graduates, when most of my colleagues had gone off to fulfill—as people of my age and status tend to do—their second (or perhaps even third!) engagement of the night. But I had no previous engagements, and, due both to Cissy and a peculiar but not unpleasant inertia that had begun to steal over me, I had rejected such invitations as had so far been offered. But if I did not resolve something soon, before dusk had entirely folded the day in its paw, no doubt I would find myself with a dry throat and an impending headache, in a distasteful and unappetizing mood, irritable and self-pitying, in something under an hour.

"At this moment, as I was considering how to reply to an invitation to accompany to dinner at a *nouvelle* Hungarian eatery two acquaintances whose company I appreciated more in the anticipation than the reality, Cissy approached me. I had not been looking at her, so the surprise and (I presume) delight on my face must have been genuine. 'My friends and I are going for a drink. Would you care to join us?' she asked me, totally ignoring my acquaintances.

"'I would like that very much,' I said. 'Where are you going?'

"'Does it matter?' she asked me forthrightly. I admired her brazenness even as I deplored its lack of subtlety and sensitivity, so alien to my own modes of approach. But perhaps she had forced herself to merely mime these latter attributes, in imitation of the kind of person she thought *I* was (knowing and self-assured), no doubt due to my age.

"'I'll be with you in a moment,' I told her.

"'Hurry, we're leaving.' And she went to join a group that was gathering by the door.

"After making an embarrassed (yet triumphant!) smile, and apologizing for what could be interpreted as a lack of sensitivity on *my* part, I excused myself and joined Cissy and her friends. If in front of my friends I had felt more proud than embarrassed by my apparent conquest of such a young and attractive being, I felt somewhat the reverse in front of hers. Although Cissy and I had been introduced earlier in the evening I was worried she might not remember my name, and was about to introduce myself to save her any possible embarrassment in this regard when it became evident she had already discussed me with them. This pleased me somewhat less than it perhaps should have, partaking, as it did, of the air of dormitory gossip. Then she introduced them to me, a veritable parade of the most popular names of the previous several decades: Jennifers and Jasons and Merilees and Cals, a Binky and Bip or two that revealed the prep school backgrounds of their possessors. One person, whom Cissy resembled only slightly, turned out to be her brother, which made my invitation to join them, if anything, more confusing than ever. As it turned out he could not have been less interested in our—or any heterosexual's—doings.

"Out of a perverse refusal to intrude myself on the younger members of the party I had eschewed, for the most part, being in the garden where they had tended to congregate, and so was unprepared for the sultry softness of the evening air. One comes across such air in the eastern or Midwestern cities of the country, but rarely in the west, where the air, in contiguity to mountain ranges, is dry and harsh. People talk about the beneficial effects of desert air, when in truth, with the sole exception of those afflicted with asthma, such air—with its drying of the protective mucus membranes of the sinus passages and throat—is by far the unhealthiest air to breathe. Did Man—and Woman too?—not arise in the moist and comforting pastures of Africa? Did not humankind—and indeed all living animals, birds, reptiles, and amphibians, not of course, to mention fish and the invertebrates—come out of the moist and comforting Mother Ocean? Do not human beings in the northern climes humidify their homes during the winter months to counteract the drying effects of heat, both to themselves and such precious objects of furniture and collectibles as their pianos and antique doll houses? Is it not, indeed, only main-frame computers—tireless and inhuman—that require the dry deadness of the air-conditioner for the healthy functioning of their beings?

"The restaurant—to call it by a finer name than it perhaps deserves—was the kind mainly inhabited by those of Cissy's friends' age and income range, and it occurred to me, not at all pleasantly, that there was a possibility that, save for the manager, I was the oldest person in the room. We sat squeezed together at a large table (albeit one not quite large enough for our needs)—a situation that only initially appears inimical to intimate conversation. With six people there is difficulty, and with eight the group—excluding the absence of a personage possessing a level of fame somewhat greater than my own—tends to divide into two usually equally-sized detachments, but if there are more than two such quartets, the possibilities of intimacy approach those of a desert island. In addition, the noise level of the 'joint,' so conspicuously appalling, in fact served to insure the utter privacy of our remarks.

"'You're an artist,' she said, in what I could not be sure was a statement or a question, for I am not totally unknown, and, indeed, only attended the party at the behest of the art director (for whom I am a kind of mentor) of the magazine the celebration of whose publication served for what Aristotle might term the Initiating Cause of the gathering.

"I always have trouble answering such a question, due to the overly self-congratulatory note the usage of such a word involves. But with a slight nod of my head and a softly-spoken 'yes' I finally acquiesced. 'And yourself?'

"'Oh yes,' she announced, in a voice that carried far greater conviction than mine.

"'And what kind of work do you do?' I asked, in a way that always sounds as if one is speaking to a child, after a slight lull in which I felt she should have asked this very question of me. But I told myself to avoid becoming petulant, not to have expectations, that just because she spoke the same language I did and had heard of and was interested in many of the same people I was did not mean that she was not of a different tribe entirely.

"'Well, it's complicated,' she began, before going into a long monologue about post-post-Modernism, Appropriation, and Political art, particularly as interpreted in the light of what Baudrillard and Bourdieu and others of that nationality had said. 'Of course you know what I'm talking about?' she said, a bit anxiously, at one point.

"'Of course,' I said, and this was true, though I had made a conscious decision three years previously to stop reading the more 'popular'—in terms of the socio-cultural milieu which I inhabit—French authors. But I had been attendant to any number of conversations in which Baudrillard had been the main topic of conversation, and in any case ideas such as his and others had been en- and dis-gorged with such rapidity and persistency by my friends that they were now part and parcel of the very intellectual environment.

"'Have you read _____?' she asked.

"'No.'

"'Or _____' and she named another book.

"'To be honest, although I am well acquainted with his conjectures, I have not actually read him myself,' I replied.

"'Oh.'

"'I assure you, in this day and age it's wholly unnecessary. We live in a transparent society where nothing is hidden and everything is known. What is truly difficult is disregarding that which it is unnecessary to know so that one has sufficient time to ruminate about that which one must. Even persons who in the past might have been considered esoteric or obscure, such as Baudrillard or Bourdieu, become transmuted by their almost instant celebrity-dom into intellectual commodities of the most pretentious, aggrandizing sort.' (Of course I hoped the use of that Marxist-type word, 'commodities,' would serve to excuse my de-mythologicization of Baudrillard and the people—including Cissy—who quoted him).

"'Are you implying I'm "aggrandizing"?' she said.

"The surface hostility of the remark was more than mitigated by her smile and the twinkling of her eyes.

"'Perhaps I wish you'd be even *more* aggrandizing,' I suggested, parrying her smile with my own.

"She blushed. 'In any case, I don't understand how can you say we live in a transparent society? The government conceals *everything.*'

"'The government conceals *nothing.* It is true, many of the reports are classified "secret," "top secret," and so on, but the contents of such reports are almost invariably publicized, albeit usually so long after the fact that the consequences of such disclosures are *de facto* nullified . There are logs, diaries, memoirs, autobiographies, and the endless memos people write to cover their. . ."butts"' (I paused before uttering the latter, as the notion of employing the plural 'asses' seemed, for some reason, unharmonious), 'not to mention computer backups of almost all of the above as well as tape recordings of even the most purportedly secret meetings. The difficulty is, there's so much information it's almost impossible to extract the essential *plotline*, as it were, from the mass of irrelevant and on occasion disinformative details in which it is invariably embedded. In illustration of this point, I'm willing to bet not one person at this table remembers the actual size of the budget deficit, though this is a matter discoursed upon on the front pages of the newspaper almost daily.'

"'Do *you* know?' she asked.

"'No,' I admitted. 'My point precisely. Do you?'

"'No. But I'm very interested in the propaganda purposes of advertising.' She turned to give the waiter her order. I could not tell whether she liked me less or more, or vice versa.

"Finding her requesting chicken in sate sauce, I mentally canceled the roast leg of lamb I had been on the verge of ordering, and instead asked for a burger. Then, as I realized such a repast was dependent on onions, I changed it to fried chicken, deciding that the avoidance of onions was of greater consequence even than even my abhorrence of resembling a person who could change his mind over something so trivial as food.

"'I should have ordered what you did,' she said, after I spoke. But I noticed she made no attempt to contact the waiter, now halfway down the table.

"'You can have mine,' I said.

"'Really?' Suddenly she became provocative in an obvious, almost movie star-ish way, propping her chin in her hands and leaning over the table towards me and speaking in a kind of breathless hush, like Marilyn Monroe in 'Gentleman Prefer Blondes'. This was touching and absurd, and no doubt the one as much as the other helped render it effective.

"The others at the table, in the midst of an apparently earnest discussion concerning the current state of the 'art world', were, with the careless insolence of youth, insulting those whose work fell into such 'old-fashioned' modes as paintings painted on canvas, drawings drawn with ink, and sculptures sculpted of metal—regardless of whether this work was abstract or representational, conceptual or expressionistic—the sole exceptions being made for those artists who 'appropriated'—that is, *copied*—the works of other artists, and/or those who splattered words or sentence fragments across their creations. 'I have many friends who are writers,' I said, 'and it enrages them that an artist can inscribe a sentence or two on canvas or metal—a banal sentence, mind you, of some philosophical or esthetic notion any writer would have contemplated (and repudiated) at the latest as a sophomore in college—and be paid fifty thousand dollars for it.'

"'Words change when they're on a canvas,' someone said.

"'It reveals the irony of the whole capitalistic process,' said another.

"'Words are more interesting when there are fewer of them,' said a third.

"'How do *you* feel?' Cissy asked me, during the lull as we waited for the waiter to deliver our orders.

"'I feel everybody is saying things they've said too often before.'

"'And your work—you must forgive me for not knowing it—though of course I've heard of you. But do tell me what it is like,' she pleaded.

"'Well,' I paused, uncertain of my reception. 'Surely you would not hold the formal qualities of someone's work against them, assuming you liked them in other ways.'

"'I hope not,' she replied.

"'I paint flowers.'

"'*Flowers!*'

"'Yes. Flowers.' I watched the varying expressions—disbelief, consternation, a tentative pass at the notion I was joking, then confusion at the same—as they flitted across her face.

"'Are you joking?'

"'Why? Is there something wrong with flowers?' I asked in all innocence.

"'What kind of flowers?'

"'Hyacinths.'

"'No, I meant. . .what do they look like?'

"'They look like. . .hyacinths,' I said. 'At least, I *hope* they do.'

"As I smiled a self-mocking smile I could tell she had decided I was joking.

"After dinner it was decided that everyone should go to a club that had opened the night before, which someone's brother was doing publicity for and who could therefore certainly get us in, preferably without paying.

"'I think I'll go home,' I told Cissy. I was worried not just about my dancing, but even more so about being absorbed into her world, rather than bringing her into mine.

"'Oh.' This surprised her. 'Are you tired?'

"'Not really. But I don't enjoy clubs.'

"'Neither do I. I live a few blocks away. You could come back to my place and have a drink.'

"Although this was her world, it would have caused what Barthes in his book on photography calls a *puncture* to have insisted she travel downtown to my loft, so I submitted to her request.

"She lived in a typical Upper West side apartment, one with many rooms, some large, some smaller, one (intended, years ago, for the maid) diminutive, a sprawling apartment whose rooms were connected to each other via long and dark hallways, a once-elegant apartment with moldings on its walls, now so far past its youth that the very doors of its cupboards and cabinets had trouble closing due to the layers of paint that had coagulated on their hinges.

"Of course such an apartment, for a college graduate, is invariably accompanied by female roommates. Two of these were in the livingroom, on an old green couch with knobby material. A boy—a young man—was with them too, astride a piano stool with his back to the piano, but his haircut and intonations were those of someone who was not interested in women.

"'This is my roommate Andrea, and her friend Karen, and this is Tony,' said Cissy. She chatted with them awhile about the party, and why, despite their prior stated intention to do so, they had not appeared, then we went into the kitchen.

"'Actually, I don't have anything to drink,' she said. 'I lied. Can you ever forgive me?'

"I felt flattered, if somewhat surprised, by her unabashed audacity. 'Only if you make it up in some other way.'

"'I can ask Andrea if we could borrow some of her Rolling Rocks.'

"'It's not necessary,' I said.

"'No. But it might be nice.'

"'Let me buy them,' I said.

"'Oh no.' But she took my five dollars and placed it on the table.

"As she stood on a stool to look for some glasses (the others all lay dirty in the sink), Andrea and Karen came into the kitchen, apparently to make some coffee, but really (I felt) to size me up. Tony followed shortly thereafter.

"'I forgot to warn you, it's like Grand Central station in here,' said Cissy. 'Let's go into my bedroom.'

"We took the beers and I followed her down a long hall to her bedroom. A double-sized mattress covered with several disheveled sheets and a polyester comforter lay on the floor next to an old bureau bedecked with an amazing array of cosmetics and perfumes—some of these in gold-flecked bottles that despite the unmistakable air of thrift shop managed to maintain at least a modicum of their former glory—as well as strands of fake pearls and earrings of presumably equally ersatz diamonds. Lined up along the baseboard of an entire wall, as if a kind of serial sculpture, were an astonishingly large number of shoes. Although these came in a variety of colors and styles and materials, the plurality, and perhaps the majority, were black in hue and had clearly been purchased from the same venue as the glass bottles and antique compacts. What caught my eye most were the heels of these leather and suede altars to the intricacies of feminine ambulation, which, elevating as nearly all did the latter part of the foot a great distance from the floor, revealed, in their idiosyncratic uniqueness, a style history from the thirties onwards of foot fashion in the larger cities of America and western Europe. When she opened the closet door to hang up her jacket, I espied even more footwear, though these were piled up in a rather more haphazard fashion. 'How many pairs do you have?' I asked.

"'Over a hundred, certainly, though I'm not sure. I often give them away to friends. But that's only an excuse for buying twice as many more.' The huge smile she radiated partook less every second of the disingenuous. For an instant I considered telling her how increasingly captivating I was finding her, but I repressed the impulse, as our roles, it seemed, had already been defined, me elusive and mysterious, her, coquettish and passionate, displaying her various wares—both immaterial and concrete—in an attempt to entrap me. By contrast women my age, confident in their careers but with an air of prickly exhaustion in arenas more personal, seemed not only far less enticing but, somehow, less sophisticated. On various intellectual and political grounds they had decried the mechanisms of desire for so long they had forgotten what it was precisely that drew men and women—or, for that matter, I supposed, women and women, or men and men, or, perhaps, even animals—to each other.

"She sat down on the mattress, and leaned her head against the wall. I sat on the edge, my legs stretched out in front of me. 'Take off your shoes,' she requested, or, rather, commanded.

"After I did as ordered, she picked them up and looked inside, holding them up close enough to smell them. They were Italian, from an expensive store in Soho, and, as so many times in the past, for reasons not necessarily identical to this, I was glad I had let my Italian friend Rudolf convince me to buy them.

"'They're very nice,' she said. 'Both the color and the feel. Are they comfortable?'

"'Very.'

"'They must have cost a bundle.' I smiled, though the truth was I had gotten them almost half-price on a summer sale. 'Are you very successful?' she asked.

"'What's "successful"?'

"She walked on her knees across the mattress until she was in front of me, whereupon she began unbuttoning my shirt. When she finished she undid my belt, unbuttoned my pants, and pulled down the zipper. 'Will you take them off?' she asked, in a tone that implied that perhaps I would not.

"I stood up and took off my pants. We still had not kissed. She put her arms around me and began to push my shirt off my shoulders. At a certain point, the shirt was pushed as far as it could go and my arms were stuck in the sleeves. 'Lie down,' she said.

"I lay down. Freed from the burden of seduction (so much less of a pleasure than it used to be that perhaps it is no longer a pleasure at all!), nothing, in light of her youthfulness, could have been more pleasant or unexpected.

"'You don't mind if I get undressed? It's very hot.' Without waiting for my answer, she shut off the light. We were only on the second floor, and the street lamp almost directly outside the window gave us a ghostly illumination. The window was open, and she stood in front of it as she took off her blouse.

"'Things are different than they used to be,' I said.

"'Oh yes.' She bent down and picked up a pair of shoes. Later on I saw that they were red, but at the moment it was impossible to discern their color. She turned slowly around, then squatted down in front of me, her breasts hanging down, larger than I had expected, making her look a little like a monkey. In a very non-empathetic way, it was erotic. But I no longer felt I could love her.

"She turned around, so I was facing her back, then leaned against me. I disentangled my arms from my shirt to reach around her to squeeze her rather large breasts, discovering, to my surprise, that unlike most women with amply-sized bosoms she seemed responsive to this form of caress. Later I realized it perhaps had more to do with the angle I was touching her from.

"It was a long time later before we kissed.

"Afterwards she turned on the stereo, one of those all-in-one players containing tape, cd, receiver, and speakers. In her small room the sound was surprisingly full-bodied, and I wondered if it had something to do with lying so near the floor (which I had not done in a long time) but when I asked her if this was the case she said she thought that was unlikely. From time to time people either in cars or walking passed by with their own radios, with stations that usually conflicted with ours, but several times played the same station, as if with an echo. The hall outside our room was dark, and I wondered if the people we had seen earlier had gone to bed, and with whom.

"'I'll tell you what it is,' she said, when I commented on her surprising aggressiveness. She began to tell me a story about her high school years, how she had dated a much older man, almost as old as I was now, although this was almost five years ago, so the age differential was even greater, and all this she kept totally secret not only from her mother, of course, but even her best friend. That is, she told her friend she was seeing someone in secret, but she pretended it was someone else, someone who was married and whose identity she had promised to conceal. Why she did this she did not know, but somehow mystery and secrecy were at the very heart of their relationship. The man, as might be expected of one dating someone less than half his age, had his peculiarities, at least in the sexual arena; indeed, that was the source of her interest in him. The good thing about their relationship was that he seemed to be able to listen to, without the necessity of evaluative thoughts either in the negative or positive direction, all the weird thoughts and desires she had never been able to confide to anybody; the bad thing was that he insisted on introducing her to new and (what at least she considered) ever-stranger sexual activities, which, although at the time she had felt (and therefore, perhaps *had*) enjoyed, she realized in retrospect might perhaps have better been eschewed. Why at an age when everything was new she had longed for such a variety of positions and attitudes she could not understand, even now. In addition to Cissy this man had another girlfriend, someone more nearly his own age, whom he saw at night or on the weekends when Cissy was home studying or out with her ordinary high school boyfriend, for she almost invariably saw this man—a designer of sound systems who worked out of his own home—during the day. One time when she was at his house his girlfriend dropped by, seemingly by accident, but (as Cissy later realized) by design, opening the door with her own key and making her presence known only when she appeared, partially clothed, in the bedroom, whereupon the man, in an excess of politeness apparently born out of his own awkwardness, asked Cissy if she would mind terribly if the woman joined them in bed. At the time Cissy did not dare to object, but in truth she had not so much minded the woman, even in retrospect, as the acts they had done that continued to haunt her. They would tie her up and spank her, or maybe they would dress her up in certain ways and enact little plays, in which she might be the shy

student and the woman her teacher and the man the princi-
pal who caught them, or perhaps she was working in a lingerie store where she would model the dresses for a special
customer who would make love to her in the dressing room
before they were caught (and blackmailed into having sex
with him) by the store manager, or she might be a little
Lolita, seducing her parents' best friends. In a way it was nice
being the center of attention, but she also felt somewhat
embarrassed by this concentration of adult energy, even if it
was just during the day and they had other, realer lives.
Sometimes she felt she should go to a shrink and once got
the school psychologist to see her, but she ended up not saying anything because she didn't really believe the thing
about confidentiality, she believed they taped everything
secretly and used it to blackmail you into behaving well at
school or ratting on your friends, and she was positive she
would be kicked out of school or her mother called in if she
ever said anything so she never did, even to her friends,
whose gossip she feared. Already she had trouble explaining
away the black-and-blue marks on her butt she sometimes
had. It was not so much guilt over what she was doing as the
absence of guilt that disturbed her. Although she told herself
intellectually that it was 'sick,' her excuse was that she knew
she would stop all this when it was time to go away to college and become the kind of person she was intended to be.
That is, that's what she felt right now but at the time she felt
she had no choice in the matter, that she had to go on seeing the man and that seeing the man sometimes meant seeing the woman, which in turn involved all that other stuff
that even now she was a bit embarrassed to think about, but
lately she had realized, after breaking up with her college
boyfriend, that that wasn't true at all, that she had been
totally free to stop seeing him at any time—the way she had
stopped seeing her college boyfriend a month ago, for no
other reason than that she didn't love him any more (assuming, that is, she ever *had*). She had never done anything

remotely like what she had done in high school with her college boyfriend, or anybody else that she had dated in college, nor had she slept with any women, though on occasion she had been approached to do so, nor had she really thought too much about it, except sometimes when she had this crazy urge to buy a new pair of shoes. Everybody in the college knew about her and her shoes.

"Less for myself than for her, because I felt she wanted— or perhaps even felt she needed—to do this, I asked her if she'd like to model some of her footwear for me. She responded with alacrity and, naked, began parading up and down the little strip of floor between the mattress and closet. There was something impersonal and practiced about the way she did this, such that the thought occurred to me she must be a professional of some sort or other, but the memory of Andrea and her friend Karen and their ambiguous friend Tony made this seem unlikely, not to mention the mattress on the floor, the fact that she was out of liquor, and so on. Not that I was nervous she was going to charge me; on the contrary, I had a strange desire to proffer her some money, both for the eroticism of the transaction and as a kind of repayment for the cavalcade of the shoes. Her legs were not especially long, and even in the high heels I could not rid myself of the notion of her resemblance to the simian, which, though this continued to make me less attracted to her, certainly made the shoe modeling progress more smoothly, for I did not try, as I often do during initial (which are often as well final) encounters, to interrupt the non-essential proceedings with iconographies meant to connote (and which perhaps actually *do* connote) affection.

"After perhaps nearly thirty minutes of this, in a pair of green suede shoes with eyelet lacing and a tall heel that widened like a bear's paw, or the bottom of a Victorian table, she rejoined me on the bed. I had slipped on my shirt so that the night air, temperate though it was, might not interact with the sweat on my body so as to provide an even more encouraging environment for the various microbes that perpetually dwell inside us. I put my arm around her for a moment and she leaned against me. 'May I spank you?' I asked.

"Did I see a smirk, or was this merely my imagination? She didn't say anything, but immediately leaned forward and turned up the radio louder. 'If you insist,' she said.

"'I do.'

"The problem then arose as to position, whether she should drape herself across my knees, or kneel down on the bed with her ass in the air and her head concealed in her arms, or ought I to force her to lean over the bureau, to see herself and her shame reflected in the mirror above it? Should I use my hand, or my belt, or a hairbrush, or, perhaps, one of the shoes? Would it be more titillating to do what I had promised, or something else in a similar vein—or perhaps most tantalizingly, do nothing at all? In short, the dilemma, which in truth confronts us at every moment, of what precisely to do, what path one should take, which road to be followed and which foresworn, presented itself to me at that moment with peculiar force.

"'And then?' someone interrupted.

"Surely the particular alternative does not matter. What is of interest is something else entirely. Somehow the presentation of myself, the iconography of my being, had presented itself to her in such a way at the party that these myths, which had lain dormant these many years, had risen up in her. And I, too, recovered certain myths which I had, perhaps conveniently, forgotten. And so we entered into a relationship.

"Now, this relationship, like others, but perhaps even more so, both due to the peculiarities of our preferences and the more banal matters of the age differential, had its difficulties. For the most part difficulties are regarded as negative in nature, but I realized shortly that, after all, this was an erroneous notion. Adversity and complications are, in fact, the fuel of our relationships, the stuff of which aspirations and dreams are made, the creative impulse behind our goals, hence our fantasies, hence our excitement, for is it not generally acknowledged nowadays that the true organ of sex is the one which lies between the ears? My triumph as regarded her age mingled with the condescension from the same in a way that provided erotic kindling for our peculiar interactions, and the hyacinths I painted, with an exaggerated naivete that nonetheless never quite managed to assuage her fear that my intentions were not sufficiently ironic, served as a springboard for many didactic (by her) and amused (on my part) pontifications on the nature and meaning of painting, art, life. . . .

"We continued in this vein for almost a year, happily reveling in the clandestine nature of our attachment, scarcely mingling with others (save, on occasions when we fiddled with the titillations of voyeurism—i.e. her roommates), all in all enjoying ourselves in an essentially guileless, if nonetheless apparently artificed, fashion. . . ."

from **Hyacinths**

An Eye For An Eye

A rally was held in support of Sam and Kirsh, who were being questioned by the police concerning the murder of James Condor. At the end of the evening Sam thanked everyone for coming, then announced that Kirsh had asked to say a few final words. Kirsh rose and went to the podium:

"I know I should get up here like Sam and thank you all for coming and giving us your support, but to tell you the truth, you make me sick! I have had it up to *here* with this bitching about society not doing this, and not doing that, and getting society to change its laws, and all that crap. . . Well who the fuck do you think society *is*? It's us, women, women who outnumber men, women who have *always* outnumbered men, women who could flush men down the toilet and say *kaput*! . . .except for a few sexual drones. . .if only we had the *guts*! But that's what we lack-the guts. All of you out there are chickenshit liberals, dumb fucking humanists. Do you think people in power just bow down and say, 'Oh yeah, you're right, I'm wrong, we've been fucking you over for the last fifty thousand years, but now we see the light and we're gonna stop?' Is this what you assholes really think, 'cause if you do you're so stupid you deserve to be the crummy slaves you are now! You want power, go take it! You gave it away, you can get it back! Men know this. Deep down, they're *petrified* of us! Why do you think they've got all those castration myths? Why do you think they try so hard to discredit the Movement, and distort history books, and call us *dykes*—as if that wasn't a *compliment*, the assholes! But we continue to be petrified of our own shadows; the idea of taking back the power we gave away *scares the shit* out of us! It's a joke. A sick pathetic joke! Let's stop talking and act! Stop cooking their meals, stop sucking their cocks, take the bankbooks they put in your joint names and get the hell out! You don't like the law; don't wait for the law to change, take the law in your own hands! If they don't want to prosecute rapists, that's fine. *They* don't have to, *we* will! Forget their fucking prisons and their whole fucked-up criminal justice so-called system! There were no prisons in the days of the great matriarchies! There were no prisons in Sumeria or ancient Israel or Greece! The Romans and the Indians did fine without prisons! Give the stupid invention back to the Quakers—we don't need it. What sense does punishment make if it doesn't fit the crime? We'll do what our ancestors did—retribution and deterrence, the *lex talionis*, an eye for an eye, a tooth for a tooth, a rape for a rape.

"Not murder, because rape is not the taking of life. Not placing in prison, because rape isn't *ex*clusion, or *se*clusion, but *in*clusion! What we want is undesired entry, forced entry, painful entry, *terrifying* entry. Make every man who rapes fear this. Let him walk petrified down the streets at night. Make him double-lock the windows of his house. Let him be scared to get out of his car. Wherever he walks, by day or by night, by the ocean or on city streets, make him walk down the streets as every woman who has been raped walks down the streets-with fear and loathing in his eyes!

"'Lynch justice' they'll call it, but it won't be done by mob, and it won't be done instantly. Two or three or four women at night, when they least expect it, silently avenging the rape of a sister. Silently, but painfully. Painfully and inevitably. Though they change their names and go to the ends of the earth, though they grovel on their knees and beg for forgiveness, though they're old and dying of disease, we will find them, and when we find them, we will enter them the way they entered us, brutally, painfully, bloodily. And when we're done, and they're lying on the ground screaming from fear and pain, with piss and shit in their pants, we will ask them how they liked it, and whether they got off, because we know deep down, despite their screams, they really wanted it! Yes, *wanted* it, the way they say *we* want it, *all* women, from *all* men, *all* the time: so we feel guilty about saying we are raped, so we feel guilty about *being* raped, so half the time we don't even realize, we *are* raped!

"Of course, we don't realize, why should we, when all it means is guilt? Guilt for being young and irresistible—and thereby tempting them; guilt for being old and unable to resist; guilt for walking alone at night—just 'asking for it'; guilt for refusing to fuck a date—because we're *teasing*. Guilt for provoking our attackers, and guilt for not fighting them off successfully: without black eyes or broken bones, how can we prove we didn't want it? Yes, if only the eighty-year-old hadn't given in to her fear and weakness; if only she had kept in better shape, she could have helped the rapist overcome his 'irresistible impulse.'

"Believe me, I *know* this guilt. I felt such guilt when I was raped, it took me ten years to remember it! Do you realize how much energy that takes, to hide something like that for over ten years? The guilt I felt, because I, a virgin, was raped by a middle-aged, balding, overweight married man with sour scotch on his breath? And a strange sick desire for a little girl, a little girl with barely any pubic hair, a girl the same age as his own daughter, a girl who had just gotten her period. A girl who didn't know what a vagina was, or a clitoris. I *still* don't know what a clitoris is. *Where* is it? What *is* sexual pleasure? Amid the filth and smells and underarm odor and hair-is that pleasure? Oh, you look at me as if I'm strange, but I'm not strange. I'm uttering the truth deep within all of you, the deepest truth of all, one so horrible we can't admit it, even to ourselves. But until we admit this, sisters, we shall never be free. Sex is nauseating . . .filthy. . .disgusting! It is the secret underlying our society, the secret behind every divorce and murder. Sex is ugly and smelly and dirty. We hate it! All women hate it! No woman, in all the history of the world, has ever had an enjoyable sexual experience! You laugh, because you are embarrassed by this truth. You cringe, because all your energy goes to repress it. It is why we are not now *All Powerful*. Proclaim our hatred of sex, sisters, and then, only then, shall we be free!

"Lest you doubt me, let us examine one of the myths of our society, the myth that is used to convince us—against all our instincts—that we *do* like sex. This is, of course, the myth called the oedipal complex—the idiotic notion that *all* children, no matter how young and beautiful, passionately desire to sleep with their parents, no matter how old, how fat, how alcoholic, how disgusting. It was a myth invented by a man, Freud, who wanted to sleep with his daughter, as all men want to sleep with their daughters, as all men want to sleep with everybody *else's* daughter! The only trouble was, Freud could see—even in the midst of blinding passion—that his daughter Anna didn't want to sleep with *him*!

"But the evidence of his senses had never stopped Freud before. All his life he had invented wondrous theories to explain why things were in fact the very opposite of what they seemed, and so he invented one now—the incest taboo! This taboo was so powerful, that the one thing children most wanted to do—fuck their parents—never even popped into their minds!

"Pretty clever, huh? Parents of the world swallowed it en masse. But sisters, *we* know better. We *know* none of us wants to fuck a sixty-year-old with green mold on his teeth, oily black dye on his hair, shit lines on his boxer shorts. What kid can even stand to look at old people, the smell and rot of death everywhere around them?

"Anna, of course, saw through her dad in a flash. He was clearly 'projecting'—taking his own repressed incest desires and laying them on her. She knew she should tell him this, but she was chickenshit, scared to open her mouth! Anna, you traitor, think of all the trouble you caused by being such a coward! But we shouldn't blame her, she was just like us, scared to tell men the truth, guilty and embarrassed. The way women are guilty and embarrassed for being raped! She felt it was her fault—for sexually provoking her own father!

"And so she never told him. The way the rest of us have never told them. Until now. *Until now.* She simply could not bear, the way the rest of us *cannot bear*, to tell men how absolutely nauseating, filthy, and disgusting we consider them to be!"

●

Daniel Beebe could barely contain his smile of satisfaction. Even the things he had secretly been indifferent to had been settled precisely as he would have wanted. He nodded, shook hands, and patted the backs of men in gray suits and white or blue shirts who were filing out of the room with black briefcases in one hand and tan trench coats over the other. The woman who had sat to the side and a little in back of him taking notes stopped to offer him congratulations, but he shooed her away too. Only the butts of cigarettes in the metal cigarette holders were left to remind him of the morning that had made him a rich man. A richer man. For he was already rich. Daniel Beebe tilted the black leather cushion against the chrome back of a chair that rested on three chrome legs set in three firm casters, put his feet on the shiny brown mahogany table, and pulled from the pocket of his jacket a long fat cigar from a country the United States did not officially do business with. When it was lit, he swivelled a half circle to face the Bay, clearly visible from his office near the top of the elongated Pyramid that was the Trans-America building. In the middle of it lay a pile of rocks named Alcatraz, where Indians used to have a sacred burial ground. White men had a burial ground there too: for those who had died in pitch-black isolation holes below ground, or were pushed off a high tier by a lover's lover, or stabbed in the back through the bars when no guard was looking, or drowned in the currents surrounding the island that would drag a man away from the city and his dreams toward the Golden Gate, China, and death. In the past, people had been glad only to leave there; after the construction of his amusement park, they would be glad to arrive. On the chopped-up rocks where convicts had sometimes voluntarily hacked to break up the tedium of what were to have been the best years of their lives, would be roller coasters, Ferris wheels, parachute jumps, bumper cars, hot dog stands, sushi bars, French cafes, and ice cream parlors—land leased from the state, but run by him. On this clear day the island stood out against the white sails of boats crisscrossing in front of it like an unpolished jewel whose value was known only to him.

Anything was possible if you really wanted it: anything.

"Mr. Beebe?"

Irritated by the interruption to his thoughts, Dan turned around to face three women. Then he smiled. He liked a pretty face—who didn't?—and at least one of the women standing on the far side of the table was pretty. Beautiful was the word. One of the others wasn't bad either, if you liked tough-looking dames. Of course, they sometimes gave you a fight.

Lots of men liked their ladies passive. But not Dan. A struggle always made the final victory so much sweeter.

The third chick, though, was strictly a dog.

"What can I do for you?" he smiled.

"It's what you can do for *us*," said the one who was

beautiful, who had blond hair. Of all the women Dan had fucked over the years, only a small number had been as attractive as this.

He smiled, then lifted his body about an inch and a quarter off his chair. "Have a seat."

But the women just stared at him. When they finally moved, it was the short, unattractive one who went to the door and turned the lock. And then just stood there.

"I don't get it," said Dan, still smiling.

"Judith Denby," said the tough-looking chick.

"I still don't get it." Dan began to rise out of his seat, but the beautiful one, the one with blond hair, walked around the table and pushed him down. Then she opened the handbag she carried and pulled out of it an automatic with an ugly black silencer at the end of it.

He did not know what was happening; he didn't move. He couldn't figure out why they had mentioned the name of Judith Denby who, after all, was just a girl he had screwed once after a party.

"Do you know why we're here, Mr. Beebe?"

"You're going to kidnap me?" Somehow in his mind he connected it with the deal he had just concluded: a very rich man.

"Hardly," said the dykey one.

"That's good." Dan smiled lamely, but the women did not smile back. It struck him that they might kill him. Anything was better than sitting there as a beautiful woman held a gun to his head, so he tried to make conversation the only way he knew how.

"So you know Judith Denby." It was not really a question.

"Yes."

"She's a fine girl. . .a really fine girl," he said desperately, trying to think of something else to say, to divert them, to give him time to make a signal, or escape.

"She's a woman. Not a girl. And she wasn't so fine a couple of weeks ago, Mr. Beebe," said the ugly one at the door.

It was weird. Sometimes the most beautiful women hung around with the most unattractive. He didn't understand it. He supposed it was pity. She was so unattractive he wouldn't have gone to bed with her in Korea, if she had been there when he was.

He was glad it wasn't she who was holding the gun.

"Oh," said Dan. So Judith Denby had been sick. So what? He didn't see why he had to talk about her with a gun at his back. He didn't see why he had to talk about her at all.

"She was pregnant."

So that was it! He fucked her, she got pregnant, women appeared in his office with guns. It made as much sense as anything else did, he supposed. It made as much sense as his pulling off that deal this morning.

Dan tried to turn his chair, but the beautiful woman with the gun in her hand put her foot up against the seat. Dan did not know what to do so he stuck the dead cigar in his mouth and chewed it as he thought about Judith Denby. What crummy luck! Of all the nights, of all the women, he had to end up with one who didn't have the sense to take pills or use the coil. Dumb cunt!

It was a shitty experience, now that he remembered it, for the first time in weeks. She had played the game a little *too* well, even getting somewhat hysterical when it was over. Chicks' crying had charmed Dan in the 50s, even in the early 60s, especially the ones who had lost their virginity. To him. But this girl—woman—was no virgin. And in the 70s, tears were a drag, they had lost their charm.

"You want money." Dan started to reach for the money clip in his pants but he felt a chop across his neck, not such a strong chop but somehow or other he did end up lying on the floor. It was as good a place to be lying as any. He couldn't believe, though, that someone this beautiful (for he had fucked beautiful women) could be doing this to him. She bent over him and lifted the money clip out of his pocket. Even though he was just lying there looking up at her he could do nothing.

She pulled the money out of the clip, counted it, then threw the clip on the floor.

"One hundred eighty."

"I'll write you a check," said Dan.

"Come *on*, Daniel." She stood over him and rather gently pushed his face this way and that with her foot. Once Dan had paid someone a hundred and fifty dollars to do just this. Now, he didn't think he could get an erection if his life depended on it. His balls clung to his body like a chimp to its mother. They strained to crawl inside where the traumas of life could no longer reach them.

"She's not pregnant anymore," one of them, he couldn't see which, said behind his back.

"That's good. I guess. Isn't it?"

"Is it?" said the lady standing over him. This time her kick was not so gentle.

"Yes," he gasped.

"Maybe a better idea would be for you not to go around sticking your cock in places where it's not wanted!" She kicked him again.

"She wanted it." Dan had only enough breath to whisper.

This wasn't fair. She had invited him up to her apartment. So he had been a little rough—lots of the ladies liked it rough! No whips or anything, basically just a psychological thing, maybe a little slapping around, to spice things up. It was the way you played that particular game, the master-slave game, and if you broke out of the part to ask the stranger you were with if she *really* wanted it that way, the game was over.

Dan did not have many free nights without his wife. He did not like his game fucked up. He was a very popular guy.

"What are you going to do to me?" he asked.

"Just what you did to our sister. Of course, we can't get you pregnant."

"You want to fuck me!" Dan asked incredulously.

"*Rape*, Mr. Beebe. *Rape*."

The okay-looking tough one walked toward him and as she walked she pulled a large, black, rubber dildo out of the huge carryall she held over her arm.

Even if he *had* raped Judith Denby, from the feminist point of view, of course (as a lawyer he knew no jury in the world would convict him of rape), still, this was crazy. It served no purpose. Trust a woman to think of something like this! He would have been glad to pay for the abortion-she hadn't telephoned him! He would give her a thousand dollars even now!—she could take a nice ski vacation up in Lake Tahoe. Or go swimming in Mexico. A girl like that was lucky to get raped!

"Take off your pants, Mr. Beebe," said the blonde, with the gun in her hands.

Dan's hands went to his belt, then he suddenly leaped up and ran for the door. It did not matter that he was risking his life. Only the ugly one the men in his battalion would never have screwed stood between him and freedom. But as he went to push her aside, she sidestepped, tripped him, and ended up sitting on his back as she reached under his body to drag off his belt so she could strap his hands behind his back. The leather cut into his skin. He did not have a hard-on. Then the beautiful one pulled down the gray pleated flannel pants he had bought in Nieman Marcus, then his boxer shorts, then she tore off his shoes. Then she pulled the gray pleated pants and the boxer shorts over his feet and off.

He was lying face down on the floor of his office, his hands tied behind with a belt, naked from the waist down.

His boxer shorts lay next to him inside out, with a brown smudge on the back. The front was yellow. Like a kid's. He jerked off in them. His goddamn ecologically minded wife did not let the goddamn maid use bleach.

As he tried to scream they shoved a thick white terrycloth hand towel into his mouth.

One of the women, he hoped it was not the beautiful one, spread apart the cheeks of his ass. Something cold and hard lay against it for a moment. Then it began to press its way in. A quarter-inch of pain, of skin rubbed raw. Dan chewed on the hand towel to distract himself from the pain. He concentrated the parts of his mind he controlled on keeping his sphincter muscle as tight as he could. His stomach contracted the way it had waiting for the snap in football. He ran numbers through his mind. His ass stuck up tight and white in the air and he could not fumble. He could feel the sweat and the buttons pressing into his chest and the sharp ache of his muscles and the dull ache of his bones. He could feel each separate hurt of every part of his body where it connected with the floor. There was a pain in his head and his jaw hurt too. But the muscles of his anus felt, oddly, good; they had never exercised themselves this way before.

The difference between this and football was that here there was no clock. Sooner or later his muscles or his mind would have to let go. As soon as he thought this he was lost. He relaxed enough to let out a fart. A loud smelly fart he wished he hadn't made. Even though three crazy ladies were forcing a solid rubber object approximately three inches in diameter into a part of his body (if an empty asshole could be considered a "part" of his body) where nothing larger than a finger had ever been before.

The relaxation of his sphincter while farting had allowed the dildo in deep enough so that further contraction of that muscle could only retard its progress, not expel it. But Dan's body pushed against it in instinctual reaction. Objects three inches in diameter and a foot-and-a-half in length did not belong inside his body! How could anybody be a faggot? An asshole was nothing like a cunt!

In addition to the soreness around the stretched tissue of the anus was a new internal kind of agony that made the pain of that muscle seem trivial. Deep within the body was a possibility for anguish he had not dreamt of. It spread beyond his rectum to his fingers and cars. It covered the red and purple spots his squeezed-tight eyes made behind his lids with a black velvet layer. It erased the difference between chest and floor, or asshole and dildo, or himself and air. There was nothing but pain. It made him want to vomit and shit and crawl into the arms of his mother, who had been dead eighteen years.

For a second he adjusted to it by pretending it was a nightmare he would soon wake up from. When that fantasy wore out, he tried another one, the black hole of Judith Denby as she had fought him off that night a few weeks ago. When that failed he let go completely and the object went into his body the last few inches. It was easy. The path of the dildo was lubricated with shit.

By now the pain was part of his life. Since there was nothing to be done, it receded into secondary consideration. All his effort was concentrated on not shitting. This effort was for himself, not the women. Shitting would be the final humiliation. Before he had tried to expel the dildo. Now he squeezed it to him. But his body might as well have belonged to someone else. His sphincter was stretched beyond all use. Inside was a mushy wasteland of indeterminate size. He had no control over what happened there.

But he hugged the black rubber object like a child. Perhaps it would stay in his body. Like a stopper.

But when Dan had accepted the state of things (the mess, the pain), the dildo began to withdraw from him. He was angry at it, as if it were a person. There was no accommodating its arbitrary nature. It intruded and withdrew, intruded and withdrew, with a rhythm that was familiar, but inside out.

Fucking was nothing like this. For in fucking you climaxed. And it was over. But this pounding could go on forever.

Dan heard his name. Someone was knocking at the door and calling him. So that was the pounding! He had to struggle up from his nightmare to hear it. He had totally forgotten about escape. It was the voice of his secretary. The one he had shooed out of the room. Her footsteps receded, came back, then receded again. Dan knew she was going to her office to get the key. In a minute she would come back and open the door like the good secretary she was. These women would jump her. But she would scream. Maybe. Then people would come and he would be safe. Maybe.

He had virtually ceased caring. As soon as he got used to something, it changed. There was no peace anywhere. He did not want to deal with anything, even his escape. He wanted to sleep for a month, then wake up in his bed at home with everything taken care of, never to be thought of again. Maybe if he shut his eyes tight enough the flowing of the dildo in and out of his body would put him to sleep.

Of course it stopped. The world was suddenly very quiet. Dan opened his eyes. The ugly one was cutting up his pants with a scissors; his boxer shorts lay in shreds at her feet. The beautiful one threw something cardboard she had pulled out of the carryall at his head. The dyke unlocked the door and in a flash they were gone.

Dan raised his head. The cardboard slid off his neck onto the floor. Someone had written on it with a black Magic Marker: An Eye For An Eye. A Tooth For A Tooth. A Rape For A Rape.

Dan tried to remember what the women looked like, but all he could see were the screaming features of Judith Denby's face.

He had to get that dildo out of his body before his secretary came back. But all he could do was the very thing he was trying most not to: shit. It squeezed out of his anus onto the horse-sized dildo; he could feel a little of the warm brown stuff sliding down his thighs.

There were footsteps and voices. In a second his secretary would be unlocking the door. The door! It was open! The women had left it open! The janitor could walk in or one of his business associates! He rolled onto his back so he could sit up, but the dildo kept getting between his ass and the ground; he had difficulty getting leverage. He knew he could do it if he had time, but he didn't, so he tried to roll to the door. As he turned, more of the brown stuff rolled out of his body and dribbled onto his legs. It was warm and soft but he didn't care. All that mattered was that open door.

He butted it shut with his head. That was one good thing accomplished. If only he could get this damn towel out of his mouth before he choked to death on his own vomit. Suddenly it was all he could think of. He didn't see how anything else could have occupied his mind. He saw the white stuff welling out of his stomach, up his throat, into his mouth, then back down into his windpipe. . . It was like applesauce, lumpy and white. . . He couldn't move his tongue even one inch, the towel was rammed so tight. There was this unbearable sharp saw (his belt!) trying to cut off his wrists. Every time he rolled onto his hands, it was like they were being amputated. . . .

Dan prayed: that it would be his secretary who would find him, that he would not vomit before she pulled the towel out of his mouth, that she would not scream before he had a chance to explain the situation to her, that she could somehow lock him in this room while she went out and bought him some clothing, that forever after she would be able to keep his secret. . . .

If anybody else came, there would be cops, publicity. Nothing—not changing his name, not moving to another city, not leaving the country—could ever erase the memory of this day. He'd rather be dead. The women might as well have put a bullet in his head.

And for what?

(A girl like that was lucky to get raped!)

The door was opening. Dan turned. Thank God it was his secretary! He nodded his head up and down to let her know he was all right. He shook it back and forth so she would know to shut the door.

What Dan's secretary saw when she entered the room was a half-naked man with his hands tied behind his back, grunting, his mouth grotesquely stuffed open, a white towel flopping out of it, a black pole sticking out of his ass, smeared with shit. The question of whether or not this was her boss did not even enter her mind.

Dan's relief at the appearance of his secretary disappeared as she began to open her mouth. He saw this slow motion, as a person drowning is supposed to see things: first the teeth, then the gums, then the tongue, then the dark hole of the throat as she began to scream. . . Which Dan, in his despair, confused with the dark hole of Judith Denby whom weeks ago, like a gentleman, he had offered to drive home in his car.

from **Some Do**

Glimpses

Marie stands by the elevator door, waiting for me. She takes my hat and coat, my handbag, and lays them by the table. She hangs my coat up. She turns to me and says "I have not seen you in a long time." She emphasizes "a long time." I move my head, staring after her dumbly. My handbag is on the table, with my hat and gloves. She is hanging up my coat.

Marie is framed by the doorway so that part of her hair is cut off by the two-inch border of the doorway. It swings out of the frame and towards the bathroom. I see my hand reach out to touch her hair, which is of medium length, brown, and soft as Ivory flakes. She makes no motion of recognition, still less of response. My hand is by my side, holding my coffee cup.

Holding my arm parallel to the floor the sun is one and a half hands above the horizon. The sun is a pale yellow ball that forces my eyes to turn away. Its pale rays lighten the blue of the afternoon sky. It is four-thirty. When I move my eyelids together there is still the impression of light, of heat, of chaos in the darkness behind them. If I had to give these bursts of energy a name, I would call them reverse sunspots. Sunspots I say out loud. Marie looks at me and says nothing. I withdraw my hand from the horizon. The corners of her lips turn upwards in a smile.

Now she is sitting in a big chair with the footrest. Her feet sit on it as they do when she is marking papers. Often I have watched her red pencil scribble on the edge of margins, erasing words, erasing students' hopes. Her hands are empty now. I am on the sofa next to the chair, I hold my coffee cup on my lap and talk unceasingly. The subjects: art exhibits, modern drama, are unimportant. The point is elsewhere, in my mouth: it is very important to keep talking. She answers with new educational methods, how my high school has changed since I have graduated. Her language is direct and un-allusive. It has a hard edge. It contains no reference to the past. I put my coffee cup on the table. I am waiting.

The newspaper says "Teenagers Terrorize IRT." I read the headline on the 135 angle the corner of the newspaper makes with the table. I find it difficult to read on the angle and I miss what Marie is saying. She looks up and stops talking. I squint my eyes but the leader is too small for me to decipher. A hand breaks the stillness of the moment: I reading, she sitting with the imaginary pencil: it is mine. I move the paper closer and read: "Old man beaten by female thugs." Her hand reaches to the coffee cup on the table. Ritual motions for the sugar. Unconscious hands. High school, students in the paper. The sharp point of the compass.

You should write a story about this she says. As always I pay close attention to her words. I do not know the this to which she refers. I am writing a story in my head as I look at her. I make mental notes of the veins in her hands, the fatness of her legs. She has brown hair and brown eyes. Her hair is long and is framed by the doorway so that the ends are cut off by the two-inch frame. Am I seeing this or thinking this. I do not know what I am doing there. Drink your coffee she says. I raise my finger to my lips. They hold a cup. I drink. Nothing comes easily, neither the thoughts in my head nor my hands as I write. Do you like writing she says? That is a question. I am not an intelligent person. I only write what I see. Right now I see myself sitting on the sofa, looking at her. Language is too allusive to describe the situation accurately. I am doing more than sitting on the sofa. My hands are waiting. They are empty. There are memories. Writing is no more than this. Describing the situation accurately. Saying only what is there. I like to write because writing brings me money and because it is not a nine-to-five job. It allows me to do things like calling up Marie and walking over to her house while the sun is still shining. Writing does not interfere with my life; it is my life.

We discuss violence in the school system. It is a problem in which I am uninterested. Buffy talks about it animatedly. Her long black hair spills out of the picture frame in back of her onto the back of the sofa. I turn my head from Marie to her, from her to Marie. I listen to what they are saying. The whole past of this recent troubled year is upon them. "High school students suspended." I have been out of the city. They are a part of the New York intellectual scene as they discuss the problem of decentralization. They refer animatedly to Jason Epstein. *The New York Review of Books*. Buffy has interviewed Rhody McCoy for the school paper. She admires him though she disagrees with much of what he does. She is very vocal. She has refused coffee and her fingers have nothing to do but play with each other. The fingers of her left hand curl into a fist. The fingers of her right hand overlap them to the knuckles. She caresses the left hand with the right hand. This process is repeated many times, then the hands are switched and it is the left hand that caresses the right hand. At the same time she does this she talks about the school situation. I turn my head to the left. Marie is looking at her. The look is familiar. I think of myself five years ago. Buffy does not have the sullen eyes I used to have, her hair is long and black. I am unable to tell how well she knows Marie.

On the telephone Marie recognizes my voice before I am able to say my name. I am in a telephone booth in the Fifty-ninth Street subway that is below Lexington Avenue. There are advertisements for "Hello Dolly" and "Promises, Promises." While we are talking a train pulls into the station. It hazes her words. It was Louis Armstrong singing "Hello Dolly" in 1964 when I was applying to college and Marie was my English teacher. There was no decentralization. It was before students were allowed to wear velvet bellbottoms to high school classes. I had never heard of acid. The train pulls out of the station. I can hear Marie clearly. I put the phone back on the cradle. I reach for the dime that is no longer there. I buy a candy bar. Marie has invited me to her home. I buy a paper. I watch for the lights of the IRT local to shine on the tracks. I buy gum.

Now the sun is lower in the sky. It has become shafts and splinters of red oxide reduplicated in the windows of the apartment house across the street. The top floors reflect a lighter, more yellow tint than the lower windows. I wonder how this is possible, seeing the sun that strikes them is solid fire. The red-orange color of the lower windows is the color of lust. I say this aloud. Buffy moves her eyes in my direction. They are a muted blue, cold, inexpressive. They reveal nothing other than the presence of the sun, for her eyelids appear slightly closer together than they would be at night. But then perhaps she is not squinting, perhaps this is the normal position of her sloe eyes.

Marie says it is strange that you should call today. I do not know what she means by strange. You call me between love affairs she says. What is significant is not the truth of this statement, but the fact that she says it. I recognize this, and am not surprised there is a sinking sensation in my left ovary. Now the sinking sensation reaches my muscles, and my heart pauses before continuing with its work. My hand rises to my brow and moves across my head in a horizontal motion. I place my fingers under my nose. I smell nothing. I move my eyes to the right and it is Buffy who is staring at me intently. I ask for another cup of coffee.

Now it is Buffy who sits by my side, swaying to some secret rhythm of her own. The conversation has reverted to the educational disorders of New York City. I consider this discussion an insult to my rank in the world. I am a writer. I live in the real world. I earn my living. I move my head to the right and to the left and to the right again. My schooldays are over I say. Education is unimportant. It is what one learns outside of school that counts. Marie and Buffy disagree with me. They say education is intimately concerned with economic advancement. Afro-Asian studies can teach the blacks to respect themselves. Integration will reduce prejudice. It is difficult to decide whether they are right, difficult also to decide whether Buffy is right in advocating revolution, whether Marie is right in contradicting her. I write my story as they talk: I note the delicate veins on the outside of Buffy's hand as she reaches down to smooth her stockings, the smallness of her bone structure and the fineness of her nose. She has a set of perfect teeth. Her black hair shines. She is as thin and as lithe as the Modigliani portrait on the wall that frames her hair.

Buffy's eyes are half-shut as she sits on the couch. The coffee cups are empty. Marie's hand fills my cup with coffee. Buffy has no cup. Marie asks Buffy if Buffy is sure she doesn't want any coffee. As hostess Marie finds it necessary to smother her guests with food. I recognize this need. I accept her coffee, her rolls. Buffy is young and violent. "Teenage Thugs Overrun IRT." It is a symptom of the times. I am more different from Buffy than I am from Marie. I say this aloud. As I stare at Buffy she turns to the wall. When I turn my head away she looks at me. My eyes are empty; they reveal nothing of what happened five years ago or why I am there today. What do you mean she says. The linearity of my mind I say. Buffy does not know about what I am talking. McLuhan, he is not with it, says Marie. I do not like him either I want to say, but I say nothing. I lift my hand from my lap; my fingers move towards the coffee. I understand Marie better than you will ever be able to. Now it is Buffy who stares at my eyes. I make sure my face reveals neither my feelings nor the fact that I am aware of her eyes. You are of a different generation I say. Your thought is non-sequential. You are taught Afro-Asian history every afternoon. You sleep with Negroes. Blacks says Buffy. That's what I mean I say. She nods her head. She is seventeen, and she sees everything. The coffee cup is halfway to her lips. It is the silence that is overwhelming.

Year by year it is harder to write. Every sentence is a fresh observation, and differs sharply from what has preceded it. There are no words to describe the flux: only an infinite sentence, without beginning, without end. Buffy is staring at me. The brain sends an impulse to the upper left corner of my lip to curl. It curls. I can see only what I write. Buffy is looking into my eyes. There is no end to writing. A story is forever.

We are sitting at the coffee table. Buffy rises to say she must go to dancing class. I say I, too, must leave, but make no motion to leave my chair. We form a tableau, Marie rising and walking over to Buffy, Buffy staring at an anonymous spot on the wall, and I pushing back my chair so that the two front legs are off the floor. We stay this way for awhile, as if life were nothing more than the eternal process of saying goodbye, staring, and avoiding each other's eyes. Marie gets Buffy's coat from the closet. She makes jokes about Buffy not having got anything for her visit. Buffy says she never drinks coffee. There is a teasing quality to Marie's digs at Buffy that signify they know each other well. When Buffy walks to the door Marie holds the arms of the coat high enough for Buffy to slip into them. My stomach lurches when Marie puts her hand on Buffy's lapel. She smoothes it. Buffy looks up at me and says nothing. She tells me it was nice to have met me. I say I hope I see her again. I am uncertain as to who gives who a meaningful look, or if a meaningful look has been given. Marie comes back to the table. Buffy is a nice girl she says. I say yes. We drink coffee.

The elevators stand in a row, to the left of Marie's apartment as you stand in front of the door. Marie's hair is framed by the doorway so that part of it is within the frame of the door and part of it is outside the frame, nearer me. She watches me while I wait for the elevator. The hall contains a large amount of silence. I can feel the silence press against the sheath of skin that is my eardrum. The drum hears nothing, reports nothing. It does not move. The elevator does not come. I look up and Marie is still there, standing in the doorway. Her hair is framed. Waves of sound press against my ear. The skin responds. You should write a story she says. I nod my head. There is the elevator, waiting for me. My feet move towards it, carrying with them my mind. My hand rests on the rubber that is the forward part of the elevator. The door bucks occasionally and tries to shut itself but my hand is stronger than the door. It is a paradigm of human will against the world of material objects. Human will triumphs. My hand relates to the door as surely as I talk to Marie. The rubber pushes my hand. I get in. Marie still stands in the doorway, her hair partway within the frame the door makes on the wall. Part of her hair is dark against the wall. I raise my hand. I will I say. My fingers float through the air in her direction. They wave as my mouth moves. It says goodbye.

Downstairs there is the doorman, waiting for me to move forward so he can open the door. He turns a face stiff with patience towards me, his hand commences a motion that he has made thousands of times before. The years of his life are punctuated by this movement of hands: the cold against his face in winter and the sun against his face in summer. He knows the house across the street almost as well as he knows the seasons. He nods to the people of the brownstone when they walk their morning dog, in the rain he whistles for them a cab. He is part human, part brick. He is a proletarian who disapproves of revolution; he tells the tenants he does not know who Stokely Carmichael is. He is a disgrace to Marx. He watches me as I button my overcoat. He stares at my left hand that has no ring. I stop a minute to adjust my collar. It is dusk.

The sky is blue now, there is a full moon over my left shoulder. The star that is a foot from the moon promises night. Leaves are against the sky, black silhouettes that knock my heart. I remember the doorman. Five years ago. I have grown up since then. I am a writer. I write novels. The sky is the same color it always was. It is as fixed as the immutable sentences. I stand and put my gloves on, looking for Buffy.

Buffy is silhouetted on the white stone of the building. She waits out of sight of the doorman; her coat is buttoned and her hands are in her pockets. She holds her books in the space between her arm and the side of her body, in the crook her elbow makes against her pocket. Occasionally she lifts her right hand out of her pocket and flicks the ash from her cigarette. It lands on the sidewalk, several inches from her foot. I am a realist. I understand why Buffy is smoking. I do not smoke, but I, too, need something to put between my lips.

I wait outside the door. I count the stars visible in the narrow space between the buildings on this side of the street and the buildings on the other side of the street four car lanes away. There are twenty-four, up and down the evening sky. The moon is over my left shoulder. I wait a moment longer, watching Buffy look at me out of the corner of her eye. She looks to see in what direction I turn. It is towards her. Her form detaches itself from the wall. Feet move. I turn and the moon is behind my back. A taxi is by the curb, waiting for me.

I hold the pregnant moment a second longer. I wave the cab away. I walk over to Buffy. I had a feeling you were there I say. She smiles.

It is later in my life that I wake up next to Buffy. Her long black hair spills out of the frame the bed makes on her body and stretches to the floor. The wind comes in and lifts a strand of hair in the caressing oxygen of spring. Buffy moves slightly, reaches out a hand which touches my breast. My body contracts. Her hand drops to the sheet and curls halfway to a fist. She is still and soft. She sleeps.

I am a writer. Most days I get up and write three pages before I make Buffy breakfast. Often we get into bed after breakfast, and by the time we get out of it the day is killed for writing. Some mornings I do not write but turn on the music and wait for Buffy to wake up. Sometimes I am impatient and wake her without waiting. I try not to do it when her eyes are moving and she is dreaming. Buffy does not like to remember her dreams.

This morning the sun is up, the sky is a bright clear blue that seems very far away and the air is fresh from last night's rain. I go over to the window and breathe deeply. I open the shades. The sun streams onto the bed, but Buffy does not move. It is a day for flowers, sunlight, and watching Buffy wake up. She breathes her young breaths. I turn on the radio. On comes a song I like. I sing along with it. The winter and the rain remind me that it's over, remind me once again that I was wrong. I think of Marie. She sleeps alone. The sun is shining. It could be raining. Buffy is sleeping on the bed. The song is wrong. It is never over.

Butch

She was so ugly I found her attractive, though of course I didn't want anybody to see me with her. When I left the bar I made her walk several feet behind me, like Chinese women used to do. I told her it was because I didn't want anybody to see me with a woman, but really it was just her-with her crewcut, what would people think? This was long before punk had made short hair respectable. Even inside my building I made her walk a flight behind me up the stairs. I was poor then, and lived in a walk-up on the Bowery. And yet I was not unhappy, for I lived entirely for love. Much of the city did then, though it never will again.

I put on a record, took out two beers and a joint, turned down the lights, and sat next to her on the couch. I felt relaxed, as I always do with someone less attractive than me, since then it's up to them to initiate sex. I would never have walked over to anybody who looked like her at the bar. And yet as I stared at her pale, soft skin, her close-cropped head, my pants got wet: amazing. A wave of total peace washed over me and I shut my eyes. The ball was not in my court. Whatever happened, happened. I didn't choose it and it was not my fault.

She began to tell me about her life. She had grown up in some small town upstate, the kind of dreary place one might look back at with pleasure, but would yearn to escape from at the time. But even in retrospect there was no pleasure for her, because her father had caught her humping her girlfriend on a sleepover date when she was sixteen and beat her up. A year later he caught them again and threw her out of the house. The girlfriend left her to marry some guy, so she moved to New York, where there were other people like her. It was during one of the lulls in the East Village, and she quickly found a share in a four-room walk-up between First and A. The normal thing for someone like her to have done would have been to become a waitress, but she wasn't attractive enough, so she took this job her roommate found her in a tee-shirt factory. They were lovers, though Diane was fat, unattractive, a real cunt. All day long they hammered stuff on tee-shirts—shiny little round things that made patterns. It was lower-class, blue-collar, real boring, back in those days before the Sony Walkman. That is, it was boring for Laura to live it, but not for me to listen to it. Everyone I knew was a struggling writer, painter, or some other arty type, so hearing her talk about something other than her foiled ambitions was refreshing.

She was supposed to be at work by eight in the morning, but she was a night person and often was late. She'd pick up a coffee and bagel and bring it into the factory. Nobody cared, everybody was in their own world. She had gotten to be friends with some of them, but Diane was jealous of anything that moved. Lately they hadn't been getting on so well; that was why she was with me now, though if Diane found out she would kill her. If Diane had walked into Bonnie and Clyde's and seen us talking, she would have beaten Laura up—and maybe me too. But luckily she hung out at Gianni's, where the serious bulldykes went, the ones who were into cross-dressing. At least that's what they used to call it, before the style seeped into the upper classes and got renamed the "androgynous look." Most of the time Diane was on the wagon, but when she got drunk she went absolutely crazy. She would push Laura up against the wall, and throw words like "slut," "bitch," "cocksucking cunt" at her. Then she would slap her. Laura was thin and soft-spoken, with tiny, birdlike bones, and I could see the pleasure one could have in terrorizing her. Once Diane punched Laura in the face and Laura had a black eye and didn't go to work for almost a week. She made up some story but everybody knew all about it anyway; they always did. Laura would tell Diane that Diane didn't love her, that Diane just wanted to control somebody. But whenever Laura threatened to move out, Diane would threaten to commit suicide, and Laura would end up staying.

"Why did you sleep with her in the first place if she's so horrible?" I asked lazily. But I knew the answer: it was similar to the reason why I was with her tonight, though somebody tall and blond and beautiful was probably lying sleepless now because of me.

"Oh, she's not so bad," said Laura.

The record was done. I thought about getting up and turning it over, but I didn't, then the silence became interesting. I was spacey from the marijuana, and I realized how tired I was of being even a little bit in charge. Of anything. It began to seem more disruptive of the mood to put on music than just let the silence be—though bits of songs played in my head like a movie soundtrack. I realized how rarely I was with another person without some kind of music in the background. I wondered if Laura was playing something in her head too. I cleared my throat to speak, but I stopped. The silence grew more and more awkward, but then, this very awkwardness should compel her to do something.

As I waited I began imagining Laura and Diane together in bed: a fat bulldyke and a water-pale wisp. The relationship was mysterious, incomprehensible, but what relationship wasn't? The tall blond woman who waited for me—my "official" girlfriend—who was she and what did it mean when she said she loved me? What could it possibly mean when I told her I loved her? What relationship did the person I thought I was have with the one sitting here on the couch, my pants wet at the idea of having sex with someone I kept telling myself disgusted me. Was it that I secretly liked her and was embarrassed by my attraction, or was it the disgust itself I liked? Did Laura put up with the fear and beatings because she liked Diane, or was it the fear and beatings that she liked?

"What are you thinking?" she asked.

"Oh, nothing." I waited a while. "Actually, I was thinking about Diane. Whether she'll punch you out when you go home."

"Does it turn you on to think about that?"

"Maybe."

Her hand slipped inside my blouse and touched my nipples. They were erect. Her hands were cold. I heard myself breathing fast, and the utter shamelessness of this—the person I was breathing fast for—only made me breathe even faster. Had I ever been more turned on? And yet, she was scarcely doing anything, barely circling the tips of my nipple with her finger. Why couldn't she put her mouth there? My body strained towards her as in a bad porno movie. She shoved her hand inside my closed jeans, though because of the tightness of the jeans she couldn't get very far—maybe a little south of the belly button. I twisted to meet her fingers, to move my pubic hairs a little more towards her. I yearned for her to undo my belt, unsnap the snap, pull down the zipper, slide her pale white fingers inside my underpants, spread my legs, drive me crazy with her icy touch. But no, she continued this lazy circling of her finger. Gradually the yearning turned to anger, that she was dawdling, torturing me by this slow tease. And yet, oddly, the angrier I got, the more my respect for her grew.

Finally she put her mouth on my nipple, undid my belt, unzipped my jeans, and slipped her hand inside my underpants. Even then, she didn't shove her fingers straight in, but kept tweaking my pubic hairs, somehow managing to avoid both my clitoris and vagina. The bottom of my body bucked in a way that was at least partly nonvolitional. Her arm pressed down on my pubic bone and I felt like I couldn't move (though of course I could). "God, you're wet," she said.

At last she pushed her fingers inside my vagina and crawled on top of me, so that the weight of her body was on the arm that was inside me. Whereas before she had been gentle, now she became incredibly rough, jerking her arm back and forth very quickly. I was so wet it didn't hurt. "I bet I could get my whole hand inside," she said, as if in a question.

"Okay," I whispered. At that moment there was nothing I wouldn't have let her do (though of course there was).

She cupped her fingers, trying to get her hand inside. It was as if I hadn't felt her before, as if my skin had been numb to individual sensations, that I'd been this wet tunnel down which something smooth had been shoved. But now I could differentiate her various fingers. "Three," then "four," she counted out loud. She had to struggle to get this last one in, and so did I. "Am I hurting you?" she asked.

"That's okay."

"If I'm hurting you I'll stop." She started to withdraw her hand. My body sucked after it.

"It feels good," I had to whisper.

"Oh." Was I imagining the triumph in her voice? In any case, she spread me wide, as if she were about to give me a D and C, then I felt her knuckles.

This really hurt, in a way that was hard to tell whether it was pleasurable or not. The tips of my nipples were no longer erect, and the wetness seemed not a response to some unfulfilled yearning but a reflex no more interesting than the turning on of a faucet. And yet I was pushing my legs as far apart as possible. I moaned when she put her teeth around my nipple. "You're very sweet," she told me.

I have always felt this to be true, though very few people have recognized it as such. With my nipple still in her mouth she pushed my jeans down so they encircled my ankles. I was sweating and messy. She was much cooler than me, almost clinical as she proceeded, which not only aroused me but made me like her better. Somehow things were more in balance than earlier in the evening. I wished she had brought a camera with her so we could have taken pictures of me masturbating to the sight of her naked body—and ever after I could torture myself over what she had done with them.

Abruptly she pulled out her hand, then I heard her stand up. I kept my eyes shut, wondering what she was doing, if she was going to search up some strange toy in her pocketbook. I heard her walk away, then behind my lids I saw, or perhaps felt, the warmer glow which I pretended was sun, but which was really a distant light in my apartment. I heard the toilet flush, but not the sound of the sink.

She came back. Her hands made me shiver. I opened my eyes. "Did you wash your hands," I asked.

"What do you think?"

They were cold, so I decided to assume she had. I lay there, the jeans still around my legs, in the same position I had been in before, as if I were tied up and couldn't move. This passivity both embarrassed me and turned me on. She took my right hand with her left and gently brought it up above my head. She held it down with her arm as she lowered her head onto my breasts and bit my right nipple.

"Ow," I moaned. But I didn't push her away. In fact, the lower part of my body gyrated towards her. She took my other hand and placed it above my head. She held both my arms down with one of hers as she crawled on top of me until her knees pinned down my arms. She pulled my belt through the loops on my jeans and wrapped it around my hands. Then she took the end and tied it around the leg of the couch.

Both the leather and buckle cut into my wrists. The belt wasn't very long and I was pulled partway off the couch. "That hurts," I said.

"But you don't mind," she said. Silence. "Do you?"

"Not exactly."

"I didn't think so." She stared at me rather impersonally, then slapped me lightly on the face.

"Ow," I said. But it didn't really hurt.

"Come on," she said. She ran her fingers very lightly down my stomach, then all of a sudden slapped me again.

This time it did hurt, but I didn't say anything. "How does that feel?" she asked.

"Okay," I said.

"Okay? Is that all? We'll have to do something about that." She slapped me again, even harder.

"*Ow*." This time I wasn't so sure I liked it. It was no longer part of my fantasy. I wasn't sure what was coming next. For the first time I really pulled at my hands to see if I could get free.

"Roll over," she said.

"What?"

"Roll over." With the belt around my hands it was hard to do this. I had to move even more off the couch and somehow turn over without falling off. Gently she ran the tips of her fingers over my ass. It rose slightly in the air, waiting for her. Whether the goose bumps were from her touch or the cold, I didn't know. I kept worrying I would fart. She stroked down the crack to my vagina, where she soaked up some goop with her finger. She used this to lubricate my asshole.

"One sec," she said. She got up, went over to her jacket to get something out, came back. With my eyes shut I waited for her finger, or maybe even a tongue (in those days before the Plague), but I felt something hard and unfleshy feeling press against me. "You ever use one of these?" she asked.

By turning my head as much as I could, I could see the black leather around her groin and the pink latex in the shape of a penis sticking out from it.

"Not this way," I said. "Won't it hurt?"

"That's up to you." She spread apart my cheeks and moved forward over my ass, then began to press the dildo into me.

"That hurts," I said.

"Just relax." She ran her fingers over my ass, and I felt the goose bumps again. I realized I was tensing my muscles, and told myself to let go. As I exhaled she pushed it in further.

"*Ow!*"

"I told you. *Relax.*" She moved a hand back inside my vagina, and in spite of the pain the wet began to flow, as if there were two separate bodies inside my one head. The other hand continued to help ease the tip of the dildo far enough into my body so that it wouldn't fall out. When I had relaxed enough to open myself to the pain, she put the hand that had been holding the dildo inside my mouth. The hand smelled like wet rubber, and I liked it. She moved her fingers in and out of my mouth in a kind of lulling rhythm; I drooled on them as if it were a cock I was sucking. Then she began to move her fingers along my gums and the muscles under my tongue, even into my nose, then back into my mouth. It was strangely erotic, though I did begin to worry about germs. With all this distraction I did not have much mental space to concentrate on the area of diffuse pain around my asshole where she was still pushing in the dildo. When on occasion I thought of it I moaned, but the pain, although intense, was made bearable by the thought of my strange submission.

Not just bearable, *pleasurable,* at the thought that all my holes were filled, my body possessed, not by just anyone, but by this being who disgusted me. Had it been someone I cared about it might have been different, but since I did not know her and there was nothing I could do about it, I might as well relax and enjoy it. No doubt I would have been happy enough with her on a desert island, where she could make love to me all day and no one would ever know. And yet, with world enough and time, perhaps I would not have wanted to let her do it, or she herself might not have wanted to do it. For is it not often true, that when you want someone to make love to you all day they don't want to, so you have to make love to them in order to get them to want to make love to you—so the person who wants sex the least generally gets more of it?

Then, beyond the pain and mental pleasures, came a powerful sensation of peace. I realized all my life I'd wanted something in there. The hand that had pushed in the dildo now cupped my right breast, as if a boat had capsized and she was hanging onto me. I was tired and I wanted to go to sleep. The sweat on my body was drying up. I hadn't had an orgasm, and I knew I wouldn't get one. "I'm cold," I said.

She kissed the back of my neck, which made me shiver even more. Then she took her hands off my breast and out of my vagina and began to push herself up off my back. The dildo pulled out a little, which hurt, though not as much as when she had put it in. "Ow," I said. But what I really felt was sadness. I had gotten used to it in there.

"Shh." She fiddled with something, then abruptly stood up. The peaceful sensation was still inside my body, but less so. When I turned my head I saw that the dildo was no longer attached to the black leather belt. She untied the end of my belt from the couch leg and lifted me up. "Be careful," I said. She was small and I was scared she'd drop me.

She carried me perhaps fifteen feet to my bed and laid me gently down. The belt was still looped around my hands and my ass still had the dildo sticking out of it. She took a blanket and placed it over me. It pressed down on the dildo a little, which felt good.

Then she crawled on top of me, turned my head to the side, and kissed me. Her lips were incredibly soft, and in spite of my fatigue I felt sexual stirrings again. "What can I do for you?" I asked. I wanted to bury my head in her, in order to fall asleep.

"Nothing."

"You sure?"

She kissed me again, then stood up and began to walk away. Again I shut my eyes. I wondered what other trick she was going to come back with-blindfold, handcuffs, tit clamps.

"Goodbye," she said.

"What?" I opened my eyes. She was standing by the bed, buttoning up her jacket.

"I got to split. You know. Diane."

Tears rushed to my eyes. Whether it was because I didn't want her to go, or because I didn't want the peaceful sensation that had spread from my asshole to the rest of my body to leave, I couldn't be sure. I began to imagine my loneliness after she'd gone. "I give the best head in the world," I said. "Haven't you heard?"

"So *that's* who they were talking about in the bar." She was so deadpan that for a moment I got paranoid. I never expected anybody I was with to have the slightest sense of humor.

"I really do," I said.

"Some other time."

She moved towards me, and I waited for her to remove the dildo. Instead, she pushed it in further.

"*Ow.*"

"That's in pretty good now, isn't it?" She patted it.

"Yes."

"I'm going to leave you like this."

"No. It *hurts.*" But the more it hurt, the more I liked it. And her, standing calmly by in her jacket, indifferently pushing the pink latex into me.

"You really don't mind, do you?" Silence. "Do you?"

"I guess not," I admitted.

"I knew you wouldn't." She gave a last shove, then bent

down to kiss me quickly on the mouth. Then she headed for the door.

I knew it could be dangerous to be left like this, my arms still tied by my belt, but I didn't protest.

"Will you come back to get it?" I asked.

" Maybe. You never know." She opened the door, then left. The words "I love you" played through my mind, although I knew they weren't true. But I felt as sad as if they were true. For a while I lay there, then I maneuvered the belt off my hands, pulled out the dildo, and went into the bathroom to brush my teeth and wash my face. Even when I was back in bed, listening to the country music station play songs from a region I wished I had been able to escape from rather than move towards, as I was doing now, the sadness stayed with me. It was the same sadness that was always there, and it occurred to me I must like it. Why else did I keep going to the bars, if not to find it?

from **_Don Juan in the Village_**

The Roof

Certain nights in the city a terrible impatience overcomes you. You look out the window and a huge orange moon is hanging there, the inside of a giant cantaloupe, if you could only reach out and bite into it, you would. But you can't, and you pace up and down your apartment, and if the night is very hot you might go up on the roof, and stare at the buildings around and below you—at least if you live in lower Manhattan like I do, where a fifteen-story building is tall enough to tower over much of the surrounding landscape. North are the Empire and Chrysler buildings, south the Municipal and Woolworth buildings and the Clock Tower, all illumined like wedding cakes, the outer-space slabs of the Twin Towers; east the Brooklyn and Manhattan and Williamsburg bridges slung out like necklaces to the lesser boroughs; west, a broad band of light—Canal Street—disappearing into the Holland Tunnel, and before that, small commercial buildings of no particular beauty where certain of the hipper movie stars now live. The tops of these buildings tend to be festooned with flower boxes, white cast iron tables and chairs, sometimes even a piece of green Astro-Turf. But all this leads me far from my story, what I saw and heard on the roof one sultry night. No excuse for this but my standard one: I am a writer, and therefore entitled to listen and dream.

It was two people from my building. Engaged as they were, they did not hear me. But I immediately recognized their voices—they were two of my closest friends, at whose apartment I have eaten dozens—perhaps hundreds—of times. It was late and very hot; no doubt this is why they were there instead of in their apartment, where the old air-conditioner was broken and the new one had yet to be installed, where no one but their dog could have overheard the deepest secrets of their hearts.

It was an argument, of course: why else would they not have heard me pushing open the door, and how else could I have heard them, perhaps twenty feet away, around the L-shaped projection of the building?

It would have been the decent thing to have made my presence known—more decent still to have quietly reopened that door and tiptoed my way down the stairs to the fifteenth floor—but what writer could do the decent thing at a time like that? Indeed, what human could, for is not gossip the glue of civilization, the external correlative of our intensive connectedness, the sign of our fetishistic interest in each other? At least so I told myself later that night when, for various reasons, only some of them due to the heat, I was still unable to sleep.

Imagine you are hearing all this under starlight, the orange moon, and the points of light of who knows how many buildings—an extravagant fantasia not exclusively for me (for surely others are staring out their windows), but a select audience nonetheless. There's the background music too, of cars, air-conditioners, subway rumbles, the residual, perpetual hum of the city, bucolic as an ocean roar, as a refrigerator, an old electric clock, and I have that peculiar reptilian tiredness when the line between wakefulness and sleep gets blurred, a kind of trance in which to stare at the hairs on one's arm is as interesting an activity as any other. I have stared at the hairs on my arm for long minutes, and I have lain on top of the bed with my clothing on, wondering whether or not to turn on the television or the radio, wondering whether it was worth it to get up and brush my teeth and remove my clothes. And I have thought about these things for hours, and not come to any decision, though the thought of the fuzz on my teeth would float to consciousness every few minutes, and after hours of wishing my clothes off, I have undressed in a flash with the lights off and my eyes closed. It was that kind of heat, my kind of weather, I drank it in up there at the top of the sky, this drugless druggy state which itself resembled a dream.

My friend began talking. She said all her life she had suffered from fantasies, fantasies which she had on occasion shared with him, her husband, but that lately, for some reason, since the children weren't around this summer, had gotten worse. She wanted him to tie her up, to beat her, to whisper filthy things in her ear, to treat her like a whore, call her "slut," "*putaine*"—she had a thing about France—his kindness, his gentleness, all the things that were good about him in other contexts (so rare & otherwise appreciated in a male)—were driving her crazy. Or maybe it wasn't gentleness at all, but some kind of horrendous sadism (she'd only just thought of this—but what a horrible thought!) that made him listen to her so reasonably, always promising to do what he could to satisfy her, but then, in bed, always stopping, after a mild slap or two. What was the matter with him? Didn't he hear her? Was he trying to drive her even more nuts than she—49, hormone demented—already was? Really, now that she thought about it, she was quite pissed (though she was making a joke about it, but don't let that mislead him!),

& that slightly bemused & quizzical expression on his face—
the look of one whose patience is being tried—wasn't help-
ing! Was he stupid, or embarrassed, or maybe he really *was* a
sadist, in the calm and reasonable way he would be a sadist,
if he *were* one. . . .

He couldn't help it, he said, it wasn't his thing. He felt
false doing it, self-conscious, as if she were about to burst out
laughing at him. Then, what if their children should
hear? What if they should pass by on the way to the bathroom
and stick their eye through the keyhole?

There is no keyhole, she said, don't you look at things
any more? The kids are gone now, anyway.

But it feels corny, like those stupid movies.

It *is* corny—the gang rape, the whore, the motorcycle
gang. But there's reason for it too, those archetypes. That's
why they're corny. Like Homer.

Homer's not corny, he protested. He had studied Greek in
college, and I knew how this must have irked him.

Oh—Achilles isn't *corny!* Agamemnon isn't a *jerk!* (she
practically spat out). And though it was absurd to be fighting
about three thousand year old literary works at a moment like
this, you had to like them for it it.

No, they're not—& what's more you don't think so either.

Oh, fuck your fucking Greeks, she said, but she said it
calmly.

It's not that I haven't tried, he said. But—I could imagine just how he lifted his hands, raised his eyebrows,
shrugged (I have imitated him doing this many times).

I know. It's not your thing, she sighed. I'm not really
angry. I mean, I'm *angry,* but not at you. Even if you could
do it *physically,* that wouldn't be enough, you'd have to—

So it's *not* the act, but something else. . . .

Don't think you're going to be able to worm out of it that
way—

Like what? Don't get excited!

I *am* excited. You think everyone has to be sane and

calm, like yourself? It *is* the act, but the act's gotta be in this. . .*context*. . . it's not just bodies doing things to each other, it's much more like a movie, not a porno movie but a real movie with a story, a scenario, a metaphor in the form of a scenario, and what it's about is, what the whole thing is about is—no matter what it seems to be about—is overcoming separateness. Maybe it's because we all started from the same cell, some amoeba, and we miss that somehow, or we're like the universe when it's time to collapse on itself. What is it you told me? Aristotle thought the planets driven by desire. . . .

That's not *exactly* what he said, he said.

Of course he was an idiot, he thought that humans had forty-four teeth, he never bothered to count them, and no one else did either for the next thousand years. At least he wasn't a fascist like Plato!

Plato was no fascist, he interrupted, and Aristotle wasn't an idiot. His voice was rising, and I knew he was losing his patience.

All right! This coming-together thing, for me, has to be done without words—I mean, words can be used *in* the scene, but they mustn't be used as explanations *for* the scene—certainly not while you're doing it, and preferably, not even now, this very discussion is destroying it. . . .

Then *stop!*

It's too late! What's exciting is that it is all done mutely, mutually, a story two people are spontaneously creating, a story unfolded, evidenced by the acts you do in bed. But the acts only have their meaning in the context of the story; divorced from that, they're nothing, a hand stupidly whipping an ass, for instance—unless of course your scenario is that of a hand stupidly whipping an ass, the hand of an idiot, for instance, your gardener, who's fantasized about you for years and finally flipped out and tied you up. That wouldn't be my fantasy, by the way, so don't even think. . . When I say "fantasy" I'm not talking about what I think people mean when they talk about fantasy—an image—I'm talking about the story *behind* the image, that which gives meaning to the image. But maybe that *is* what people really mean when they talk about fantasy, who knows? people use language so imprecisely now. It can be anything, of course, even something that looks like what I think people are talking about when they talk about fantasy, for instance, a story that two people are fucking in a way that is like an image in a glossy magazine, a totally superficial fucking with no history except two bodies glistening with oil—but that's the scenario, two bodies without history fucking in oil in front of a photographer who's going to put the photos in the story is the meaning of that story.

But we're not strangers, he protested.

That's the problem. I'm a woman who likes to paint, and you're a man who supports me by selling computers.

For a long time they were quiet. It's a hot night, he said.

Yes.

I've got my fantasies too. I've always wanted to fuck on the roof, under the stars, with the lights around us, never knowing if someone up there (he must have been referring to the tall building directly to our north) might have their lights out, watching. Would you like that?

Talking about it ruins it, I've told you.

I should just jump on you and pin you down?

Jesus! I imagined her exasperation—with his literalness, with his confusion of language and "meta-language" (though she would not have put it in precisely that fashion—though *he* might have—if he had only been aware of what he was doing. But if he were aware of what he was doing, he wouldn't have been doing it, would he? Unless he *were* a sadist. . . .)

Actually, he said, I agree with you. Deep down, of course, I'm just a kid. Strip.

What?

Strip.

There are moments you feel that you know everything, that the loves and desires and fears of the people before you are as transparent as those inexpensive plastic watches in which all the works are visible, and other times you feel you know nothing, that you're a stranger on a planet of alien beings whose every gesture repulses you—and sometimes you feel these both at the same time, and empathy makes war with the deepest disgust. That's the way I felt now, as if I knew them completely but not at all, and some of what disgusted me attracted me, and vice versa, and then I realized that if I felt this way towards two such close friends surely friends of mine would feel the same towards me—perhaps even these very two friends. . .and a rush of horror washed over me—and I mean *washed*, drenching my body in sweat (but perhaps I *was* ill, why else was I up on the roof eavesdropping on my friends?) that I should even once be seen in the same light in which I now realized I routinely viewed others. . . .

That's not what I meant. You're not supposed—

Ow. Could that have been a slap?

Shut up.

But—

Definitely a slap. Do you realize what you sound like? You. . .you. . .you. . . kids this, kids that, everybody comes to me & wants everything when deep down *I'm sixteen & I don't know dick. Now strip.* I pay for your clothes, now take them off.

But—

Somebody could *watch*? So let them! Like we don't own our apartment? Like someone's gonna throw us out of the building for a morals violation! Move it. When I'm angry I get a hard-on.

Jerry! A laugh, but a nervous one.

A really loud slap. I'm not kidding.

Whimpering, a long silence, sounds compatible with a shoe being taken off, another, a zipper being unzipped. I saw her, my friend, naked on the tar, stretch marks, a little overweight. (But of course, I could be imagining all this. For all I know, they're playing a tape—a tape of an argument, a scene from a play.)

On your knees.

I can't, my knees.

Fuck your knees. I'm tired of your knees. Your life is your knees.

Like a dog I saw her (my friend!) kneeling, her stomach hanging down, her hair over her shoulders, the sweat where her pants had circled her waist, a rim of water on her hair, etc.

Spread them.

Jerry—

Spread them. A harder slap. You wanted it, now you've got it. . . .

Not *this*. Perhaps I heard noises, suction, perhaps I imagined it. Come on, Jerry, it *hurts*. Not *there*.

Shh. Hold still now, a little. . . .

I can't, really. . . .

Uh.

Jerry—

Uh!

I imagined Jerry, overweight himself, too many beers, wet with sweat, his knees aching from the tar, the little pebbles embedded in them, that would stick when he got up.

Ow! . . . Ow! . . . Ow!

Then, a little later, as the ows get softer & fall into a kind of rhythm: come on, tell me how good it is, how much you love me.

Fuck you. I hate you.

Like you mean it.

Grunts, suction sounds, strains almost like machinery creaking. If I could leave, I would. But how can I? I stare at the stars. My mind wanders. Perhaps I'm embarrassed. Perhaps I'm remembering things. Then the noise level peeks and I realize, after all, that I waited too long to leave.

There's the quiet after, the slowing of the breaths, then—

That was great, Jerry. Thanks.

Thanks? For what.

You know. . . .

No. . . .

Come on. For, you know, doing what I told you. . . what I asked you. . . I know it's not your thing but—you could have fooled me. . . .

Fooled you how.

Pretend—

Pretend nothing.

Silence. Huh?

This is who I am.

Jerry—

This is who I really am. You just never saw it.

Okay, have it your way. Irritation again. Scrapings of shoes, zippers.

I will.

You know, you're really giving me the creeps. . . .

Really? Why? Sounding so reasonable, I imagine her trying to decide whether to slap him.

You *shit!*

Standing up. Do you hear something? Pause. For I had tripped slightly in my haste to move backward.

A long silence, as everyone holds their breaths, surely not wanting to know, as I tiptoe back around the corner of the water tower, a place they do not even glance towards at as they cross the roof to the door that leads downstairs. I stay behind the water tower, disturbed and superior, long after the sound of their steps vanishes, until what I imagine is the elevator comes and goes many times, until a light in the room under the skylight clicks off, until even a clock on a building across the way dims. . . .

And as I go downstairs, as the elevator passes their floor, I wonder how I'll relate to them, now that I had this knowledge, the knowledge that is power, but also shame.

I had trouble falling asleep. I reproached myself both for not leaving the roof, and also for not stepping closer so I could see them. Yet I could see them as clearly as if I had watched them.

I shut my eyes and fell into the fog I had been in for days. Neither awake nor asleep, stories paraded through my mind, desires long concealed, disgusts overcome, persons I had never thought of as sexual objects doing unspeakable things to me, stories where the normal was bizarre and the bizarre normal. . . .

I had witnessed them, yes, but that meant nothing. What was important was their scenario, and this was something I would never know, whether this was a one-time having to do with hormones and weather or merely a version of the way they ordinarily made sex, insult followed by insult, some white-collar imitation of a blue-collar guy and his dame, a hodgepodge of scenes from the old movies they liked so much. Who would have guessed it? but the slap was real, I'd heard it, more than once, and the "ow" that followed. But no matter how much I analyzed it, I'd never know, I could only imagine. Even if I asked them, they could lie.

But perhaps my friend didn't know either, whether this was the "Jerry" who was performing his duty to a hormone-crazy wife, or a "Jerry" who had flipped out due to the heat, or the "real" Jerry who only now was able to come to terms with his deepest desires. . . .

Maybe Jerry didn't know either.

And I realized this was true, not just of what we did in bed with the people we slept with, but everything in our lives, stories we invent with our friends, relatives, the guy at the gas station and the gal in the supermarket, your lawyer, your realtor, your accountant, your doctor, the airline pilot and the ticket taker, the fellow from the IRA who audits your account, the taxi driver, the bum, and the guy who drinks his coffee instead of selling you a subway token— to explain why this event happened and that one didn't, why we felt good yesterday and bad today—as if we're scientists and there's something to discover, rather than artists collaborating on creating a world congruent to the one that we've been making up in our heads.

But maybe this too is just another story, words spun up to give shape to an August night when it's too hot to stay in your apartment. . . . ?

"Total Time"
at the Kiev

"God, those are gorgeous!" screamed Judy that afternoon in the Unique Clothing Warehouse, re a skintight pair of pink spotted leopard pants. "Can anybody lend me fifteen bucks?" she asked.

"They are *so* gross!" said Karen.

"Isn't he cute?" said Elissa re a stock boy who was straightening out a pile of jeans.

"Yuck!"

"Excuse me, sir, do you have the *total* time?" Saralee asked a man out in front.

"That lady gave you *such* a look," Judy said to Saralee outside.

"I fooled her," said Saralee, holding up a Day-Glo orange plastic watch she had slipped in her pocket.

"That's nice," said Judy.

"Here. You want it?" She gave it to Judy.

Elissa and Karen had put their names down at the Astor Place haircutters to have a haircut, so they went back to wait on line while Saralee and Judy headed for the Kiev, which they had heard of as kind of a punk luncheonette. "Two Cokes," Judy told the waitress. While they were waiting for the Cokes a young Puerto Rican boy asked if he could share their table. There were several Puerto Ricans in Judy and Saralee's school, but not many, so of course this became an interesting encounter to them. In truth, any unknown boy, of whatever nationality, would have provided an interesting encounter.

"What's your name?" demanded Judy.

"Julio," he said.

"I'm Saralee."

"I'm Judy," said Judy.

"They don't let you sit at a table if you come in by yourself. A coffee please, " he told the waitress. He took out a book and started reading it.

"Actually, I'll have a coffee too," said Saralee.

"Me too," said Judy. They waited for the boy to speak but he continued reading. "What book is that?" Saralee asked.

"Just some computer stuff."

"We have computers in school," said Judy.

"Apples?"

"Yeah. "

"We've got PCs," he boasted. "I'm trying to disprove the red shift."

"What's that?" asked Saralee.

"It has to do with how fast the stars are moving away from earth. I don't think it's as fast as most scientists say. If this is true of course they're not as far away either, because time and distance are the same. The reason I think this has to do with what Einstein says in the theory of general relativity, that gravitation is indistinguishable from acceleration, which to me indicates that the red shift could be measuring not acceleration but the gravitational curve generated by a finite, curved universe. As Einstein said, if the universe is curved, you could send off a light beam from your eyes and it would eventually come back to the back of your head. So the star might look like it's coming from there" (he pointed north) "but it's coming from there" (he pointed south). "You follow?"

"Not exactly."

"Nobody does," he said. "My teachers tell me I'm a genius."

"Everybody in our school is geniuses," said Judy.

"Where's that?'"

"Uptown," said Saralee, kicking Judy under the table.

"Do you go to public school?" Judy asked.

"Yeah, but I'm going to go to a good college. Not that it matters. Einstein didn't go to college."

"He did *too.*"

"He did *not.*"

"He did *too.*"

"No he *didn't.*"

"You want a refill, kids?" asked the waitress. They all bristled at the word "kids." Then they broke up laughing and Julio closed his book.

"A friend of mine's brother just got this VCR. You want to go there and watch a movie?"

"Where is it?" asked Saralee.

"Just down the block."

Saralee and Judy looked at each other. "Sure." They left the Kiev and started to walk up Second Avenue. Saralee chattered away but Judy was worried. She had never done anything like this in her life. She had heard of many young girls like herself who had been sold into slavery—by Turks, of course—but what if this dark-skinned boy's name wasn't Julio, but Ahmed or Mohammed? She walked along the street, her head down. Saralee nudged her in the ribs. She pulled herself up tall and straight—not "straight" as opposed to "gay," but "straight" the way girls from Nightingale-Bamford walked, an invisible shoebox filled with cocaine, which they must not drop, balanced on top of their heads. A stone lay on the sidewalk, but she did not kick it into the gutter, though she longed to.

The apartment was dark, with what looked like an old Indian bedspread covering the window. Saralee immediately plopped down on the floor as if she were at home. Judy was uncomfortable. She wandered into the john, then got a glass from the kitchen. When she returned to the living room Saralee and Julio were laughing together in a way that seemed to exclude her. A pang went through her—her first in this connection. But she saw it as iconic—it would always be like this, three people, with the other two liking each other and her out of it. That's what being an only child in a family was all about, wasn't it?

"Is *Back to the Future* okay?" asked Julio. It was a rhetorical question, as he and Saralee were already fast-forwarding to a favorite part. Once the movie started he went to a drawer and took out a plastic bag with what looked like oregano in it. "Oh good. Marijuana," Judy said, super-casually. Very carefully he rolled a joint. Judy had tried pot a couple of times at parties with ninth- and tenth-graders, but never alone in a room with a boy, even though the boy wasn't with her, but with Saralee. Saralee acted real cool, she held the cigarette like it was no big deal. Judy, impressed, decided to imitate her. She prayed she wouldn't cough, but she couldn't help herself. To her relief they didn't laugh at her, but probably that was because they weren't really interested in her, but in each other. She peeked through the bedspread covering the window to the street. Diagonally across was an old church, with some grass around it. This green, in the midst of these ugly old buildings, somehow seemed more interesting than all of Riverside Park, which she and her friends wouldn't play in after school any more because they were grown up and interested in different things. When she turned around, Julio was sitting with his arm around

Saralee's waist, Saralee's head against his body. They looked happy, like a TV ad, like people she didn't know. In their bodies, somehow, was the secret of perfection. Judy knew she didn't have it, would never have it. It was unfair, but who was there to blame?

"What are you mooning at?" asked Saralee, giggling. She felt embarrassed, to be sitting there with this guy as Judy watched. She wondered what Judy would tell their friends. She wasn't sure if she really liked Julio, or was merely grateful he had chosen her over Judy.

"I'm *not*," said Judy. Despite herself, a petulant stubborn edge was in her voice. Whenever she heard herself sound like this she felt fat, like an old woman with a big red nose. Her voice sounded peculiar in her ears, as if she were hearing it in a different way than usual—through the bones in her body rather than through the air. Teeth made good antennas, she has read in some book. Or, at least, imagined she has read. The idea of teeth sticking out of the top of the World Trade Center made her giggle.

She sat down and tried to think normal thoughts. Julio's friend came in from across the hall. He was fifteen, taller and scarier than Julio. Just looking at him you could tell how cool he was. Actually, Judy liked Julio better; maybe because he seemed safer. The boy sat down next to her.

"Where do you go to school?" he asked.

"Columbia Prep."

"What's that?"

"Oh. Just some school uptown."

He soon lost interest. He got a pillow from the couch and put it under his head. There was nothing Judy could think of to say to him. Meanwhile she watched Saralee and Julio kiss. They seemed to be doing it the way you saw in movies, with the mouth open.

"Okay," said the boy. He turned toward Judy, touched her arm. A chill went through her. Goose bumps rose on her skin.

"Do you have a sweater?" she asked.

The boy laughed, gently pulled her down to him, then kissed her softly on the lips. It was nothing like a spin-the-bottle-type kiss. Judy actually forgot about Saralee. She was both embarrassed and excited.

"Let's get some privacy," said the boy. When he got up and started down the hall to the bedroom Judy followed him. The last thing she wanted was to make a fuss. Obviously she was doing all right, better even than Saralee. He sat down on the bed, kicked off his shoes. Judy just stood there, staring at him.

"What are you waiting for?" asked the boy. Dutifully, Judy sat down on the bed and took off her shoes.

He put his arm around her shoulder. Instead of kissing her as she expected him to do he pulled her down on top of him. He smelled different from normal boys, almost sweet, as if he were wearing suntan lotion. She had no idea what she was supposed to do, or say, or not do or say. The last time she had been on a bed with a boy was when a bunch of kids were playing some stupid board game, back in elementary school. Since then they had gotten self-conscious and couldn't do things like that. His lips on her neck gave her more of the same kind of chill she had before. It was almost unbearable. He put his tongue in her mouth. It was fat and wet, kind of disgusting, though she wouldn't have admitted that to anybody. She tried to push it out with her tongue, but he pushed back with his. She got her tongue behind her teeth and clamped her jaws together so hard she began to get a headache. She could feel his tongue moving around her gums, a peculiar, almost ticklish feeling. She prayed he would stop. Then he rolled on top of her. He put his hand on her leg and pushed up her skirt. This felt so strange that to prevent it she opened her mouth in a trade-off; if she did this maybe he'd leave her leg alone.

He put his hand higher on her thigh. She couldn't help herself, she gave a little jump. He pressed down on her and she felt something hard against her leg. "Could you move your wallet?" she asked.

The boy laughed. Then he rolled onto his back. "How old are you?" he asked.

"What difference does that make?" asked Judy.

He laughed again. He leaned up on his elbows and opened the night-table drawer and pulled out a pack of cigarettes. He lit one with a blue transparent lighter, then leaned back on the bed. He looked like a god out of the movies. Matt Dillon, Sean Penn, somebody like that.

"What are you, in the eighth grade?" he asked.

"Yup."

"You go out with guys a lot?"

"Well, not all *that* much. " She spoke as if she were embarrassed about the "not that much," when the truth was more like "not at all."

"I can tell," he said. "You call me up when you get older. Okay?"

"Okay." Judy would have loved to ask him what she did wrong, but the embarrassment of having to listen to the answer in his presence prevented her.

When he finished the cigarette he sat up and put his shoes on. Judy did the same and followed him into the living room. The VCR was on with the sound down. Saralee and Julio were listening to Simple Minds. Saralee gave Judy a look. "We gotta go," she said.

"Yeah," echoed Judy.

The boys didn't say anything as she and Saralee got themselves together. Judy wondered if she should remind the boy to give her the phone number.

"Bye," Saralee told Julio.

"Bye." They kissed. The boy Judy had been with was in the kitchen. "Hey, look, I don't remember your name," she told him, when she went in to say goodbye. She pretended to laugh.

"Paul," he said. Judy waited for him to ask her *her* name, but he didn't. She wanted to tell him her name was Judy but was embarrassed to do so without his asking. What if he said "What are you telling me that for? Do you think I give two shits?" She wanted to ask for his phone number, but was scared he wouldn't give it to her. She herself could (under)stand it if he did this, but what if he went out and said in front of Saralee and Julio something like "Do you believe it? This girl wants me to give her my phone number?" They'd all howl on the floor and laugh at her. "Come on," Saralee called.

"Well, we're going," said Judy. "Goodbye."

"See you around."

"Where?" Judy was on the verge of saying, but thank God didn't. She walked slowly out of the kitchen. He was emptying ice out of a plastic ice-cube tray into a plastic ice-cube holder. A dark god playing with ice.

Saralee and Judy were silent as they hopped down the stairs to the street. Outside, Judy turned around and looked at the number on the building.

"If you walk up three flights does that mean you're on the third or fourth floors?" she asked Saralee.

"Whatdjew do? Get laid in there?"

"Boy, are you dumb!" replied Judy. Actually, she wasn't too sure of the precise meaning of the word *laid*. People seemed to use it like "screwing," only the image she always got was a hen, sitting on top of a bunch of eggs. "We just frenched a bit," she said.

"Us too. Then he wanted me to feel him down. Ugh!"

"Gross!" agreed Judy.

"Like, have you ever been so hungry?"

"Like. . .like. . .no."

"Pig-out time!" they shouted in unison. First they ate a pizza, then a souvlaki, then they got ice cream cones from the home-made ice cream place. Then they wandered into a record store that sold old records, mostly by groups they'd never heard of.

from *Real Estate*

Faithfully Yours

Although I have long acknowledged, at least to myself, that I don't live for pleasure, it is only recently that I have been forced to admit that the mental tortures of regret and recrimination lie so profoundly at the core of my being. Perhaps, even, *are* the core of my being. I will tell you, in brief, how this realization came to pass.

Picture a conference—you've been at one, I'm sure—filled with writers, or aspirants thereto, of the American variety, fiercely competitive, rabidly jealous, anxious both to secure a piece of the decreasingly sized pie for themselves and to prevent it from reaching the mouths of others. There are two thousand of us, or more, in a hotel in Boston, which is both a city and the dream of a city—a colonial city of the British Empire, horizontal, with parks and low skyline—a city where the taxi drivers still speak English and know how to get you where you are going. The skin of the people is white. Not an American city, after all.

I paid the taxi driver and carried my bags into the hotel. Stuffing the receipt into my pocket as I went through the revolving doors my attention was somewhat divided, so that I emerged almost stepping onto a soft carry-all someone had deposited right in front of the door. I was about to say something snotty to the boy in the baseball cap who was bending over to pick the bag up by the strap, when I realized it was not a boy but a woman. She was wearing jeans and a light brown leather jacket and her baseball cap was navy blue. I was wearing a dark blue baseball-style cap myself, though mine was wool rather than cotton. My hair was shorter than hers, and my height lesser, and my age greater. I watched her walk to the elevator, where she joined a group of people, one of whom was doing her best to look like a man, though she was really too short to pull it off.

From the back, I realized her hair was long. She looked nothing like a boy.

I believe I've neglected to mention that it was not just any ordinary writers' conference, but the Perverse Writers' Conference. All writers' conferences are boring in their way, but the Perverse Writers' Conference perhaps less so than any other, for there is sure to be a very oversized man wearing rollerskates, and a very short woman who insists on smoking a cigar, and a whole host of people who are furious because the Physically Abundant have not been provided with extra-large seats, and that perfume (so distressing to the Allergically Impaired!) is not absolutely proscribed. Even our tee-shirts—'I Lost It at the Movies' (Pee Wee Herman whacking off); '10 Things a Man Can do Better than a Woman (Rape You, Beat You, Give You VD, Forget to Pay Child Support. . .)'; 'Anything Worth Doing Is Worth Doing Badly' (two bored-looking women doing the Unimaginable)—are superior. We are talking, in short, about the kind of a group where the only people likely to be found in the health club are women.

My bag was light so I managed to carry it to my room. It was a big room with two beds, perhaps too big: the television was so far away you would have had to sit at the little round breakfast table to see it. The radio was part of the television system and you could not turn it on from the bed. The bathroom had a hair drier (which I had brought) and many towels, but no shower cap, shoe horn, shoe polish, body lotion, cream rinse, telephone, or complimentary robe (none of which I had brought).

Before taking a shower I called room service. After a long and unsatisfactory discussion about available decaffeinated and herbal teas I ordered some hot water and lemon. Then I lay down in the water to take a long, skin-drying bath (there were no bath oil beads or bubble bath either). The skin on my fingers would shrivel into lizards, but what did it matter? No one would care but me, and I didn't count.

Why didn't I 'count'? I have been pondering this my entire life and still have not found a satisfactory answer.

The door knock came as I was still ruminating. Hurriedly I pulled on a clean shirt (it got wet) and, with a towel around my waist, answered the door.

But it was not room service. It was my friend Barbara, who had the room next door. "You weren't answering your phone," she accused me.

"I'm taking a bath. Where have you been?" She raised her forearm so it was at a right angle to her upper arm and tensed her extraordinarily large bicep.

I settled back in my bath. Barbara turned on the TV and continued her post-workout stretch. The sound of college basketball played pleasantly in the background while I tried to space out. It seemed much safer to do this with Barbara in the next room than it had been when I was alone. It is often more enjoyable, if less exciting, to be with someone one is not in the least attracted to. When the knock came and I heard Barbara's voice asking "Who is it?" I suddenly thought: what if room service pulls out a gun and shoots her? I shivered. (Of course, for I was in the now lukewarm water.) Barbara brought me in some tea and I drank it in the bath, but despite the warm liquid inside and outside (I turned the hot water on again) something in me was still cold.

As I was trying to figure out what to wear, the phone rang. It was my lover. Whereas an ordinary lover would have called to say she missed me, or hoped I liked my room, or was having a good time, my lover was calling to tell me how happy she was to have the apartment to herself, the cat to herself, the kitchen to herself, the sofa and bed to herself, the VCR and the three movies she was planning to glom out on to herself.

I told her that I suspected much of her pleasure was in informing me of this.

She laughed, and asked if I was having a good time.

"Not yet," I said, "but I think I will."

"So the women are beautiful?"

"One is," I said.

She told me she was going to shut off the answering machine when she began her movie orgy. Therefore if I called her and didn't get an answer I should not get paranoid.

I instantly got paranoid. To make myself feel better, I went into specifics about the person in the baseball cap.

"Good luck," she said. As always, she sounded like she meant it.

I had, of course, considered being unfaithful to my lover, and to that end had brought along my sexy underwear. To whom, at a conference of the Perverse, would such an idea not occur? My lover and I had had many illuminating and enlivening discussions on said topic, without ever having been able to come to a definitive answer. Almost anything I discuss with my lover gives rise to an illuminating and enlivening discussion, as she is vocal, intelligent and perverse—not just in the sexual sense but every way. I say this not out of partiality but in the interests of veracity. Indeed, I am not at all sure that the ability to discuss subjects interestingly and intelligently is a positive attribute for a relationship. (Certainly it is not something I ordinarily value—indeed, it is something I have often gone out of my way to avoid. Amongst other things, it is often extraordinarily fatiguing.)

What we came up with was this: fidelity was certainly impossible—in the theoretical sense—but unfortunately infidelity, though Platonically desirable (indeed, how could one find love in the midst of a relationship save through infidelity?), often foundered in practice, due to various weaknesses and fallacies of the human psyche, contingencies that even we ourselves (however superior we considered ourselves to be) might on occasion find ourselves prey to. We therefore assumed, in the contingent sense, an unarticulated but mutually observed discretion, and, in the Platonic sense, an only partly ironic expectation of the 'worst'—which, in the context of our peculiar relationship, might be the 'best'—as this assumption seemed to prolong the intensity of our sex life beyond what might reasonably have been expected.

I do not attempt to defend our peculiar relationship. All I can say, by way of exculpation, is our perverseness has less to do with choice of sexual object than with a shared infatuation for contradiction, complication, and other allures of the enigmatic and obscure.

One might go so far to say that, whereas in most relationships sex commences where the rational ends, in our relationship it is the sex that is rational and the conversation where the truly 'perverse' commences.

The idea that my lover was happy because I was away perked me up (as no doubt she had intended it should), and with this renewed confidence I was of course able to choose what, for that moment in time and the current state of my hair and skin and mood, was the 'perfect' thing to wear.

Overhearing all this, and observing my mood shift, Barbara assured me I was crazy.

But in her room, watching her change out of her sweatsuit into something if not much dressier then at least cleaner, overhearing her half of her conversation with her lover Lucinda (rather, *ode,* for surely its forms are as codified as any sonnet's, replete with "me toos" and "I miss you toos" and little smacks of the lips at the end), it struck me that it was Barbara's relationship (and not mine) that was crazy.

I am not sure when it became impossible to be 'natural' but probably sometime before it became *de rigueur* for people like us to wear baseball caps.

As it turned out, Lucinda hadn't come to Boston, not for honest perverse reasons, like my lover, but because she had a sore throat. Lucinda always had a sore throat when Barbara did her thing.

The cocktail party was large. The cocktail party was noisy. The cocktail party was filled with people drinking club soda fogged up with little squirtings of lime. It looked like abstinence but it was really the far side of indulgence, and I felt like a child with my silly wine spritzer.

The baseball caps were gone, replaced by dresses or man-styled suits—for the distaff side of the room. Some of the 'real' men wore jackets, but many just wore sport shirts and pants, or even tee-shirts and Levis. If someone had really short hair, the odds were at least even that it was a woman rather than a man.

I was amused to see that some blacks were still wearing dashiki-type outfits, and that a certain kind of woman dressed as boringly as she might have in the late 1970s, to prove that a certain kind of 'seriousness' will never go completely out of style.

I said hello to the woman whom I had been unfaithful to my lover with at the last Perverse Writers' Conference. It had not been a wholly satisfactory experience, at least in retrospect, because once my lover told me she did not find her attractive I realized I didn't find her attractive either.

We kissed each other on the cheek and told each other how well we looked. In fact, she did look well, mostly due to a little slip of a cocktail dress she was wearing, very unlike the wool pants she had worn last year. I realized my outfit (black stretch pants, fake leopard boots, black jacket) could have been one I wore last year (in fact, very likely *was* the one I had worn last year), and my confidence immediately evaporated.

The rest of the evening I spent trying, like everybody else, to find people who would tell me how great I looked and what a wonderful writer I was.

I looked for the woman in the baseball cap. Either I could not recognize her without her cap, or she was not there. I did see her short fat friend. But then I saw there were other short fat women around the room, and the more I looked the more I did not know which of them was the right short fat woman.

A normal person would have come to the conclusion that if you could not recognize someone without her baseball cap she could not be that attractive to you. But the way I looked at it was: it was my duty to uncover and recapture the mysterious kernel of attractiveness that had been kindled by the iconographic use of my favorite (at least to read about) sport.

I continued to search for the woman in the baseball cap all the next day—walking out of panels in the middle and catching only the final minutes of others, looking for that telltale headgear in the back of rooms or at the entrance to others. Even while I gave my own little speech my eyes anxiously kept working the room.

In this state of mind, of course, it was impossible to pay attention to the conference.

It was how I always acted when I had a crush on someone. Barbara kept telling me how stupid it was, but, as usual, I found it somehow 'witty'. It was all I could do not to call my lover and tell her about this. She was the only person in the world who would have understood.

No matter the state of your heart, it behooves you to eat

dinner. I had been pestering Barbara to go someplace expensive and exotic to eat, but she wanted to hang around the hotel with some people she had run into earlier.

"Oh, all right," I said grouchily. I was sleepy, sick of everybody. Or maybe it was just a sugar depletion fit. I kept flipping the plastic pages of the three-ring looseleaf tourist book the hotel had provided with brochures of various places to go to eat and things to see, without being able to come to a decision.

"Come on," said Barbara.

She wore a jacket of denim over a vest of denim over a shirt of denim. For some reason it made her look more femme than when she wore a skirt. Watching her as she tied, with admirable lack of indecisiveness, a red bandanna around her neck, I grew more and more nervous about who I was, particularly in relation to the question of lipstick. I went into my room, smooshed on some make-up and gel, and put on a cowboy shirt.

It looked terrible, though last year it was great. I put on a black GAP tee-shirt, but I felt like an older person trying to imitate a twenty year old, so I took it off. I put on a silk shirt over the same stretch pants I wore the night before.

"What are you doing?" asked Barbara.

"Trying to get dressed."

"You're fine. Come on."

"I'm not fine." But there was nothing left except a little black mini-skirt which my lover had insisted on slipping into my valise, and which I certainly could not put on so early in the evening (and most likely not at all), so I followed Barbara to the lobby. With every step I took I felt, for some reason, more and more like a transvestite.

Sitting with the people Barbara had arranged to meet for dinner was the woman in the baseball cap and her friend who looked like a man. I was happy they were there, and unhappy because of the silk shirt.

I placed myself opposite the woman in the baseball cap and ordered a burger, not so much because I wanted one as to show I was not 'politically correct' and would still eat meat.

Barbara's friends were discussing 'butchness' and 'femme-ness'. The woman who looked like a man had come up with a series of categories into which all women—at least all women like us could be divided. According to her theory, there were fourteen different ways of being a 'butch', and fourteen different ways of being a 'femme'. Certain kinds of butches would appeal to certain kinds of femmes, and vice versa, but other kinds were a 'must to avoid', kind of like a horoscope.

The different categories seemed to be determined not, as I had always thought, by how you were in bed, but by your haircut, your clothing, the way you walked and talked and came on to people in a bar.

The more she said the more nervous I got, and the more self- conscious about my silk blouse.

"That's all arbitrary," I said. "I often force myself to do things differently than I used to."

Ah yes, she said, you could do that. But you could never really fool anybody. Because underneath your actions and your speech and your make-up and your clothing, there was something instinctive and unchangeable: for instance, the way you organized the different parts of your body, or where you held your hands when you weren't doing anything in particular with them. Just as, despite my gold earrings and my silk blouse and my fancy shoes, anybody could tell I was butch. Even if I wore high heels and a skirt, I was butch.

"But I'm passive in bed," I said. Everybody laughed.

Everybody was staring at me. My hands were on my hips. Embarrassed, I took them from my hips and placed them on my lap. Then I became embarrassed about being embarrassed, and tried to sneak them back on my hips.

"You see," she said, "you can't help that."

"Yes I can." But a little later I caught myself with my hands on my hips again.

I leaned forward and began eating the pretzels on the table, just to have something to do with my hands. I finished several bowls before the food arrived. The burger was thick and difficult to eat; the lettuce and tomato kept falling out, and occasionally a glop of ketchup. The others were all eating vegetarian cheese or yogurt type things. They finished before I did, then sat there calmly, apparently unworried about what to do with their hands when they weren't eating.

But whoever we were and regardless of where on the appearance dialectic we made our stand, we all listened intently to our man-tailored philosopher. And the difference that began to seem truly significant was not whether we wore jeans or skirts, silk blouse or tee-shirt, but that we were having the conversation at all. What seemed truly alien was the waitress, whose every gesture signified innocence and unself-consciousness—despite the fact that she was wearing too bright red lipstick and an outfit that, with its short skirt and low-cut top, surely was meant to be 'sexy' (although I doubt whether any one of us would have found it so). You could only get away with dressing like that if you did it with the proper degree of irony. But the waitress was so unironical she did not seem to notice any of us as being 'different' from her.

As she took away our plates, the woman who dressed like a man (her name was 'Connie', but her girlfriend called her 'Con') again began talking about femmes, but the waitress did not hear.

Or if she heard, she did not react.

Or if she reacted, it was not visible.

Perhaps, after all, a waitress (or a waiter), can never be visible. And that is why it is often so difficult to remember which one is yours when you want your check.

Meanwhile the woman in the baseball cap said very little, her only sign of nervousness the cigarette she suddenly asked Connie to light.

When she inhaled the bottom of her nostrils flared, and I felt I was watching a 1940s movie in which the detective finds himself in love with a girl who pretends she is in love with him but is more likely just leading him on.

"I didn't know you'd gone back to smoking," Connie said.

"Just for this weekend," she replied, "or Roberta will kill me." She glanced up and saw me looking at her, then turned her head away. In profile, I saw the line that demarcated the part of the visual universe that was her face from the part of the visual universe that was the background glowing with a soft white light, presumably from a light source behind her head. A cloud of white formed out of the two funnels of white she blew from her nostrils and dissolved upwards in the air. I may have been deceived, but it seemed she was doing it all for me.

Because it was suddenly okay for me, despite whatever I wore, to be butch, because I suddenly knew, despite the baseball cap, she was a femme, I smiled my slit-eyed smile at her, the one you see on my book jackets, the sleepy-looking one that is both natural and artificial. It was directed first at her eyes, then at her breasts, then I ostentatiously moved them further down to where the edge of the table cut off the rest of her body.

"Are you going to the dance tonight?" she asked.

"Yes."

"Are you wearing what you're wearing?"

"No."

Due to my evident confusions, Connie suggested coming to my room and dressing me. I tried on all my outfits, including the little black mini-skirt. Under her gaze, my clothing no longer seemed ambiguous and subtle, but a sign of cowardice and confusion.

Looking at myself as an object of desire rather than as the one desiring, I wondered which of the fourteen types of butches—the ones who were tomboys and the ones who were punks, the ones who were 'daddies' and the ones who were faggots, the ones who were 'mamma's boys' and the ones who were jocks, the ones who were cowboys and the ones who were sluts, the ones who were 'stone butches' and the ones who masqueraded as femmes, and all the other kinds I could not remember—I was, but I could not tell.

Although I had worn my black jeans on the train and did not consider them 'dressy' enough for the dance, Connie insisted I wear them. She kind of liked the man's shirt I had brought to wear under a Perry Como-esque sweater the next day, but she said it needed something else to make it dressier—like a tie.

"I don't have a tie."

"*I* do."

She told me to leave my pocketbook behind, and stick my money and the plastic card that took the place of a room key in my shoe. Sometime in the past I had done this, perhaps in high school, following a sweaty-palmed boy onto the dance floor. Going to her room I felt the excitement I had then, of pretending to be something I was not, even though what I was pretending to be, this time, was myself.

Connie changed out of the suit she was wearing into another, equally masculine one, but of somewhat lighter material. She took a shirt off a hanger in the closet. It looked exactly like a man's, but it had been tailor-made especially for her, because her neck and wrist length and breasts made it impossible for her to wear a man's shirt off the rack. The shirt had black and gold studs instead of buttons, and cufflinks to match.

I fingered these. They felt substantial and real, part of the same world in which I hid my money in my shoe. Once I bought my father cufflinks. I used to like looking at them in the little box which was not just a box but a kind of home for them—in the sense a cat box is a home—with its little padded throne covered in a kind of fuzzy bluish-grey material. That kind of jewelry seemed so much more real and intelligent than my mother's. But now cufflinks and suspenders seemed anachronisms no longer worn by men, but only by women such as me.

Instead of putting on her shirt, she handed it to me.

"I can't wear this," I said.

"Why not?"

"It's too nice. What if I spill something on it?" She looked at me. "It's just not me," I said.

"It *is* you. You don't really think silk shirts are you, do you?" I put the shirt on. Then Connie lay several ties around my neck, to see which worked best with the shirt and my skin coloring. We settled on a black-on-grey silk one. It felt substantial too, and real.

It was me, of course, and it was my father. And she was my mother as well as my father as she knotted the tie around my neck.

Then Connie's girlfriend Sandy came into the room and told Connie how great I looked, and that Elaine (the woman in the baseball cap) would be sure to think so too.

I felt like a man overhearing female gossip.

Connie made me brush my hair to get rid of the gel, then rubbed some shiny man's hair cream on it, so that it was slicked back like a 1940s gangster, or Pat Riley. Usually when my hairdresser did stuff with my hair I felt as if she were trying to make me into something I was not, but Connie seemed to be bringing out the essence of who I was. As to whether or not I liked this person, I was not sure. She finished it off with a dab of Brut.

I looked at myself in the mirror. In it was a woman who was clearly a woman, but a woman who was attempting to get at something that was the essence of a man. Perhaps because it was false it seemed more like a 'man' than a 'real' man did.

Back in the lobby it took me a few seconds to recognize Elaine. She was wearing a silvery latex mini-skirt and matching top through which the curves of her ribs and the convexity and concavity of her chest when she breathed were visible.

"How did you get it on?" I asked.

"Talcum powder."

I had never seen latex in any color but black or red or green before. The silver shimmered softly, reflecting the hotel lights like an inviting pool you might fall into. On her head she wore a black hat with little dot conglomerates stuck here and there on the veil. My mother had worn hats like this once, but I hadn't seen one, outside of the movies, in decades.

Connie's girlfriend wore a black tube dress. Other women surrounded Barbara and Connie and me in their miniskirts, their spandex jumpsuits, their lingerie tops, women who in the day looked just like me. It was like discovering a new world, but one that existed not instead of but behind the old one. This made the old one seem not less but more interesting.

Those women looked at Connie and me, too, as if we were concealing a mystery, one that had to do not just with studs and cufflinks and ties and the smell of man's cologne, but something stranger and sexier. I could see it in their eyes. I had the power.

I wanted the power. I wanted them to swoon at my fucking feet. I wanted to be the heterosexual male rapist. I wanted to be a faggot and have them suck my cock.

"Shall we dance?"

I led Elaine, in her strange little veiled hat, onto the dance floor.

You know how people dance: they stand apart, they shift their legs, they tilt their heads from one side to the other, they snap their fingers, they rotate around themselves like the moon, they revolve in circles around an imaginary center located somewhere between themselves and their partner.

Every time I revolved back to a certain spot, I saw Barbara looking at me. I knew what she was thinking: I was a phony, not a real butch at all. But I was doing as well as if I were a real butch.

I stopped to buy Elaine and Connie's girlfriend a beer. Then Connie bought me a beer. Barbara wasn't drinking.

Elaine stood talking to me. The veil hung so far down that she had to slip the bottle under it to drink. The veil hung between the bottle and me, and I yearned to push it away.

We talked as we drank, and though she looked at other people, she stayed with me. She told me about her life in the small town in which she lived on the other side of the continent, with children she had had in an earlier life, and the woman she lived with now, and the ways in which it was good and the ways in which it was not. And the more she talked the more vivid that far-off life in California became, and the less vivid this real life in Boston. And as her life in California became more vivid, so did my own life in New York, until I knew that if we did not start dancing soon it would be too late.

I knew that if she would dance with me again, she would sleep with me. I put my hand, lightly, on her right hip, as I led her to the dance floor. Ever so subtly, she leaned her hip into my hand. But when we reached the dance floor, she began to move away, into that solitary dance where we rotate and revolve around ourselves.

It wasn't me. For years I had forgotten, but the shirt and tie made me remember—even if, years ago, it had been someone else wearing them. I pulled Elaine to me, and with my right hand on her left hip, and my left hand holding her right, I began to lead her in a version of a dance you call the lindy.

I drew her towards me. I pushed her away; I spun her around under my arm, one way and then the other; we put our left arms behind our heads and slipped away from each other till our hands caught; face to face we held hands and brought them up and over our heads and, still holding hands, rotated under them; we danced side by side, my left arm around her; and we danced with my front to her back, in sync.

It seemed like the real dancing, the dancing I had done in high school, before people stopped dancing with each other and started dancing with themselves. Only then I had been the one being led, and not the one leading.

But the leading came naturally, like the shiny hair goo and cufflinks and tie.

And when we were not doing any of the above, I held her left hip next to my right one, and with my left hand on her right, twirled her around and around in circles that were both rotations and revolutions, faster and faster so that I became a fifteenth kind of butch, a Fred Astaire kind of butch, and the people around us stopped dancing, stood in a circle, and clapped.

It was my finest hour. When you are a Fred Astaire kind of butch you can have anything you want, and you should.

I looked for Barbara. She was gone.

The lights were wrong. They wouldn't dim. The one by the bed was the least bright, but it was magnified by its reflection in the mirror over the dresser so that if you were lying on the bed it glared in your eyes. The light on the dresser was brighter but further away and because of the lampshade didn't reflect in the mirror. I opened the bathroom door a little, but the lights were fluorescent. There was a hanging lamp over the little table where I ate my room service breakfast, but lying on the bed you could see the bulb underneath the shade.

The furniture was dark, shiny, the top covered in a Formica pattern of imitation wood. The people who invent this stuff, the people who market this stuff, and the people who buy it for hotels have done a vast disservice to millions of people all over the globe by insulting their eyes and their brains.

Elaine had refused to accompany me to my room, but told me she would sneak up after she had said good night to Connie and Sandy. For the sake of the lover back home in California, she was maintaining the appearance of fidelity.

For the sake of my lover in New York, I did not want to maintain the appearance of fidelity, and this upset me.

I took off my shoes and lay down on the bed. But I did not want to pull the covers off the bed, and the bedspread, shiny and quilted, was cold and slippery. I stood up, smoothed out the bedspread, and walked over to the little breakfast table.

I felt short, very un-Fred Astaire, without my shoes, so I put them back on.

I fiddled with the radio stations. It was not New York. I could not find what I wanted. I settled for some 1970s music. Once offensive and jolting, it was now played on the 'soft rock' station.

What could I do while I waited? A book or television would alter who I was at this moment. I did not want this, as Elaine liked who I was at this moment. Then it occurred to me: if I were to read my own book, I would only become more of who I was.

But when I got it out and looked at it, the words I had written, about a character who was me, seemed to have nothing to do with me. I remembered writing the words, but not the feelings.

I looked up the hotel movie guide, and ordered something from the 'adult' channel.

These movies are all alike. Women stroking each other in that soft way that is the only way men can imagine women have sex, and a man watching, waiting to reap the results of all this preparation.

I unzipped my jeans and began to touch myself, but I'm not sure if I was actually turned on, or just trying to be turned on. I took off my shirt. It might be interesting if I answered the door naked, except for the tie, as might happen in a porno movie. But my stomach looked big in the mirror, not butch at all, and the breasts seemed to contradict the iconography of the tie. I buttoned up my jeans and put the shirt back on, but left it open, my breasts half visible, the tie hanging loosely down over my collar.

Fifteen, twenty minutes went by. The phone rang. There it is, I thought, she's not coming. I felt both angry and relieved.

But she had only forgotten my room number.

Before Elaine entered the room, she took the 'DO NOT DISTURB' sign from the inside knob and put it on the outside. "Of course, Connie and Sandy figured out what I was doing," she said.

I wanted to kiss her, but instead I said, "The lights are fucked." She got a towel from the bathroom and put it over the lamp, so the glow was diffused.

"How'd you know that?" I asked.

"I've made love in hotel rooms before."

She looked at the TV a minute and said she had watched that movie the previous night, then she lowered the sound. She took off her shoes, then her hat and her veil. I will not insult you by telling you the irrelevant color of her eyes. It was too dark to see anything in them.

"I want to kiss you," she said.

I had brushed my teeth, of course, but the beer was still in my mouth. As I opened my mouth, as I stuck out my tongue, as I let her tongue brush the inside of my mouth, I was conscious of this.

I was so conscious of the taste of beer in my mouth I wasn't conscious of the taste in her mouth, not even whether there was toothpaste or not.

Our mouths went towards each other. We were standing. We did what we were supposed to do. Then, awkwardly, I pulled her on top of me onto the bed.

I looked over to the movie. A man was entering a woman, from behind.

With her on top of me, I became confused. Was I supposed to be a man or a woman?

I put my mouth on hers. I knew where it was supposed to start. I knew where it was supposed to go. I knew what I was supposed to feel.

"I love you" went through my mind, though of course I did not mean it. Lately for some reason, I had been unable to feel desire without these words parading through my mind.

My lover's image was in my head. I pictured myself in bed with her, telling her about this night. She would be turned on, by the dancing and the latex outfit and the hat.

"You seem far away," Elaine said.

"No."

"I can feel it."

"That kind of remark only makes me further away."

I kissed her again, but she wouldn't open her mouth. In my head I saw how a man did it, unbuckling the belt, unzipping the pants, slipping the fingers up the skirt.

If I opened my eyes I would surely see some similar movie scene, without having to invent it. But that seemed more difficult somehow.

"Tell me what you're thinking about," she said.

"I can't."

If she had been my lover I would have told her, and the thoughts that were going through my mind would have amused and excited her. But I did not trust her to be amused and excited. I felt she would get angry and leave the room.

She moved off me. She lay on her side next to me. I propped my head on my elbow and looked at her. She was very attractive, more attractive probably than my lover.

I felt that to kiss her, to really kiss her, I would have to open myself up in a way that would erase my lover from my mind.

"I really like the way you look," I said. I traced the outline of her lips and her nose with my finger. People did this in movies. But still, I was not turned on.

We tried to kiss again, then we lay there awhile. I shut my eyes, and fell asleep for a tiny part of a second. Her words woke me. "Maybe this isn't such a hot idea." I giggled, at the word 'hot'. "What are you laughing at?" she asked.

"That word." She looked puzzled. "Hot." She didn't laugh. I wasn't sure whether it was because she didn't understand or because she didn't approve. "You're probably right," I said. I felt bad, and wanted to do something to make her stay. But in order to make her want to stay I had to do the thing that was the reason I wanted her to stay, and this was what, despite my conscious inclination, I was unable to do.

"Are you often like this?" she asked.

"No." This was true, although it seemed like it could have been, in fact should have been, a lie, and that it was only by chance it wasn't. My lover would have understood.

I did not want to make love with my lover either, but grow sleepy talking to her.

I thought about talking about all this to Elaine, but it seemed too complicated. My perversities might be able to charm a person of leisure, a person without children, but not a person of responsibility, a mother.

"Why don't we just go to sleep," she said. "Maybe we'll feel better in the morning."

I watched her get undressed. Like a mother, she folded her clothing responsibly, whereas I flung mine on a chair. We both left our underpants on. There was a terrible silence after the TV was turned off.

As scared as I am of desire, I'm scared of the lack of desire more.

In the dark it would be all right. In the dark, where no one could see anything, the tendrils on my arm would surely wake themselves from their embarrassed slumber and tremble to desires once forbidden. In the dark, under the surface of my actions and my speech and my make-up and my clothing, where no one could see the way I organized the different parts of my body when I was not doing anything in particular with them, would not my hands, my feet, my breasts, do what, in days gone by, they had always done?

Of course, with the shirt and tie off, I was a different person than the one she had liked.

I put my arm around her. She turned away, so I was hugging her back. I moved my hands up to her breast, but her arms guarded them. "Shh," she said, though I had not said anything.

Almost always I have trouble sleeping. The window of opportunity is small, the distractions great, the consciousness of the difficulty involved the greatest hazard of all. I thought about all the other times I had lain in bed, unable to listen to the radio or TV or turn on a light to read, next to women who were somehow able to breathe deeply and sonorously, even after a scene like the one Elaine and I had just had. Usually they were what is referred to as 'normal'. As suspect as my motivation is, so is theirs.

The longer I thought about it, the angrier I got. After about twenty minutes or so, I realized my pants were wet.

I put my hand on Elaine's shoulder. "Could you put your hand inside me?" I asked.

She shook me off, but I repeated the question.

She rolled over. "Could you put your hand inside me, just for a few minutes?" I repeated. She sat up and turned on the light. She looked at me as if I were some vaguely repugnant object. Then she swung her legs from under the sheets to the carpet.

I sat on the side of the bed watching her as she got dressed. I had no talcum powder and it took her quite a while to shimmy the latex back on.

She put on her shoes then walked to the door. "I'm sorry," she said.

"I'm sorry too." I felt empty and sad, as if it were a long relationship that was ending.

I left the door open till she turned the corner. First I took the 'Do Not Disturb' sign off the knob, then I put it back.

I couldn't sleep. I never can when I drink. I took aspirin, vitamin C, water. Elaine's face never left my mind. I'd been unable to have sex with her because I kept thinking of my lover, and now I was unable to sleep because I kept thinking of Elaine. I would think of her, I knew, the next night in New York, when I lay in bed next to my lover and tried to have sex with her.

In the past I have always had the conviction, that what I was doing with a woman in a room was the most important thing in the entire world. My mind still had this conviction, but not my body.

I yearned to call my lover to discuss why this was no longer the most important thing in the world, and also what was, but the phone machine would not be turned on for many hours.

We had arranged to meet at ten for breakfast. I'd liked the idea of showing up for breakfast with Elaine on my arm, sleepy-eyed and satisfied. As it was, I went downstairs with Barbara. She seemed unduly pleased by my recounting of my failure.

Elaine was already at the table, a little pot of *espresso* before her. She made room for me next to her, and we politely kissed each other on the cheek. Barbara looked at us as if there was something the matter with us.

"What happened to your baseball cap?" I asked. It was the first time I had seen her in public without something on her head.

"It was Connie's. I gave it back before I forgot."

So she, too, had been dressed by Connie. We were, both of us, imposters. It made me both like her more and feel less attracted.

In between bites of toast and eggs, we discussed what had (not) happened. Despite my contempt for people who live in northern California I decided to try to do this. "Sometimes I have trouble responding when I'm supposed to," I said. "I keep having these conversations in my head with my girlfriend. Maybe I should have told you. Also, I felt you only liked me because I was wearing Connie's shirt."

She looked at me as if I were crazy. "Who likes people because of what they're wearing?"

"I do," I admitted.

"You mean, you liked *me* because of my latex outfit?"

"Don't forget the cigarette," I added.

It wasn't the truth—at least not entirely—but I wanted her to think it was, so she'd get angry, so I could apologize, even if what I was really sorry about was something else.

Of course, even as we were talking, I was having another conversation in my head, with my girlfriend. It seemed a much more interesting conversation than the one I was actually having, and yet all I was doing was reciting to her the details of my conversation with Elaine.

Connie and her girlfriend arrived. I was hoping Elaine hadn't yet spoken with them, but immediately they started in with the jokes. At first it bothered me, then as I drank more coffee I began to find it amusing, for the more they talked the less and less Elaine and I were who we were and the more we became these characters in a story, a somewhat perverse comedy of manners whose subtext was subtle and complex without being in the least pathological, which partook nothing of abuse or incest or any of the other generic explanations about people like us. The 'me' character in this story was provocative, ironical and enigmatic, and although I happen to consider myself provocative, ironical and enigmatic, my character in this story seemed to embody those characteristics in a wholly different manner than the way I thought I did.

It was kind of like high school, where you spend all your time talking about your friends, but if so at least I was in the 'in' group, and I decided it was okay. Better than okay. "Fun."

When I said goodbye I kissed Sandy first, then Connie. I had planned an extraordinary gesture for Elaine, a Fred Astaire kind of grasping and swooping backward, but she must have thought I was going to skip her entirely, for she pulled me toward her as I was still moving away from Connie, so I had no time to prepare my histrionic kiss, and had to give her an ordinary one instead.

It began to snow before we left the station, First it was late afternoon, then it was twilight, then it was night. It reminded me of something. . .good. . .long ago, on the train with the snow coming down, Barbara and I and the others in our comfortable seats speeding past the towns of Rhode Island and Connecticut where normal people lived. I wanted to be them, for a week, maybe. No. Less. For the length of a movie of their lives.

The soundtrack, against the snow and the houses and the stations and my face reflected in the window as it grew darker, was a conversation with Elaine and my lover, as overheard by Barbara. I was explaining myself to them, first my desire to feel, then my fear of that desire and how that fear made it impossible for me to feel, then my embarrassment about all this, my desire to have this understood and forgiven and, most of all, be loved in spite of it, which was surely the greatest desire of all, as well as my only hope of salvation.

Elaine and Barbara and my lover looked at me as I talked—the me who was not just 'me' but a character in Connie's story—and the houses sped by and the snowflakes got bigger and the sky grew darker and my face was reflected ever brighter in the glass, and as I spoke my voice grew softer and softer until my lovers and friends fell under the spell of my words. And as long as I kept talking I knew I could have them all, *for ever* (and anyone else, of course), and the more I realized this the more I was able to feel—by which I mean my pants got wet—and I became a normal person, just like you.

The Ontology of Post-Modern Sex

I was recently asked to be on a panel discussing how I wrote about what is called "lesbian sex" for what is called "the mainstream." As I have little imaginative ability—I am averse to inventing so much as the color of my characters' eyes—I quickly realized that the way I wrote about "sex" was similar to the way I wrote about any subject at all: i.e. I tried to remember as much as I could about it and then to transcribe both my actions and *the sentences that occurred in my mind* while I was performing these actions, as faithfully as possible.

But this led me down another, more interesting path—which was, why did I choose to perform the actions I did during sex and not other? For certainly, out of the vast repertory of sexual activities and positions available to me, certain ones I abjured as inevitably as I embraced others. More than that, I tended to perform acts in certain sequences (often, I am forced to admit, in a kind of "progression" I theoretically deplore), and it was not at all clear to me how I decided to stop one activity (e.g. sucking a breast) and switch to another (e.g. "going down" on someone), or was it even "I" who made that decision or was it "just my body"? And why did I sometimes have sex, or even *initiate* it, when I wasn't in the mood and other times *not* initiate it when I *was* in the mood? And then I began to wonder what it meant to "be in the mood," and why one tends to get upset if one hasn't been "in the mood" to have sex for a period of time (I may *wonder* why I'm not in the mood for skiing, or going to the movies, but I don't get *upset* or go to a shrink about it), and then I began to wonder whether I even *meant what I said* when I said I "enjoyed" sex—because at times I enjoy it when I *don't* come and sometimes I don't enjoy it if I *do* come—which led me to the question of whether enjoyment was really the point after all—because we don't have to think and analyze and go to shrinks in order to do the things we *know* we enjoy doing (like skiing or going to the movies)—but whole industries (psychotherapy, porno, and prostitution being only the most obvious) have been organized solely around dealing with the problems of sex—which is not the case for other pleasures (save food and the various legal and illegal stimulants, of course).

But whereas the difficulty with these other problematic pleasures revolves around questions of increasing addiction and concomitant difficulty of withdrawal, the problem with sex is that its "addictive quality" vanishes so quickly—at least in relation to one specific person—and frequently not just the addictive quality of the desire, but desire *at all*.

But if we do not have sex for pleasure, why do we do it?

Some of the reasons: because we think our partner wants it, because we want to be thought the kind of person who enjoys it (even if—or *especially* if—we're not), because we feel that sex is necessary to establish a relationship, or maintain a relationship, or even *demonstrate* a relationship—though to whom I don't know (but perhaps to oneself. . . ?).

Needless to say, this is is not the realm of eros. Needless to say, this is not the position one started out from, in the Golden Days of Slut-dom. It is, however, the position of the *self-conscious* or *ironic* or *post-modern slut* (whereas some are born to slut-dom, and others have it thrust upon them, still others have to seek it) who approaches sex with the dedication of a scientist and the soul of a Puritan—in search of gnosis rather than pleasure.

●

When I think about sex, I experience a kind of empathy with Freud, who was always asking *what do women want?* I'm not referring to *other* women here, but myself. Because not only do I often not know whether I want sex or not, or whether (when I'm having it) I'm enjoying it, but even when I *know* I'm enjoying myself I'm still not always sure I wouldn't rather be doing something else. My mind wanders, and it didn't use to, or when it used to wander, it would wander to things like: "I wish she would do that," or "I wish she would go slower," or "I think I'm in love with her" or "I wonder if she loves me"—but lately, even when I have found myself in bed with someone I thought I wanted to be in bed with I have sometimes found myself unable to concentrate enough to even have sex—and I'm talking about someone *new*, now (not someone familiar and boring)—which in the past, regardless of whether I particularly liked the person, was a situation I always enjoyed and got excited by, if only in an egotistical kind of way.

What are the kinds of thoughts that go through my mind now when I'm having sex? Well, what I *most* fantasize about is the sex being over, and being able to do something else—like read or watch tv or get something to eat or go to sleep or talk; often I fantasize *talking* with the person *about* sex (as sometimes, when I'm talking with the person, I fantasize about *having* sex)—and I often fantasize, for some reason, about telling my shrink about sex and how boring and unsat-

isfying it is (I smirk as I do this, and she gets appalled!).
Sometimes I even *fantasize about telling her about how I fantasize about telling her* about the boring sex. Are these
thoughts sexual or not? I'm not sure. Then sometimes,
because I'm a writer, when I notice my mind wandering I tell
myself to concentrate on the sex, not so much to enjoy it, but
so that I can remember what's happening so I can write about
it—i.e. *write about why I'm not enjoying it*—and this having
to remember gives me a purpose, so that there's some "reason"—other than "pleasure"—to keep doing it. I mean, sex
takes work, both physical and mental, and then you aren't
expected just to *do* things, you're expected to *enjoy* doing
them and having them done to you, and if you don't do you
have to give explanations about *why* you don't enjoy them—
which is *also* work. Not to mention something very anxiety-
provoking. My life is already filled with anxiety, so why would
I want to add to it? All things considered, sex is no longer
really "pleasurable" for me, it's more of a kind of duty in
which, if it works out relatively well, I am more relieved than
happy, though I *do* look forward to the moment *after* it's
done, when I've experienced whatever pleasure I'm going to
experience and my mind often goes foggy and I fall asleep or
into a trance. But, unfortunately, the moment *after* pleasure
isn't the same if one doesn't *experience* the pleasure *first*, so
in order to achieve the happiness *after* pleasure I try to get
myself to experience pleasure (by doing certain breathing
tricks and concentrating etc.) but this is really more of a *duty*
to have pleasure than an actual pleasure. Should pleasure be
a duty? Is pleasure that's a duty really a pleasure?

If sex were *really* a pleasure, I think, I wouldn't have to
try so hard, I could just experience it.

●

That this problem isn't idiosyncratic just to one neurotic
writer is clear from the phenomenon known as "lesbian bed
death"—the widespread inability of dykes in relationships to

maintain sexual activity. "Bed death" isn't exclusive to dykes—gay men and heteros have it too—but it seems a much greater (and certainly more discussed) problem in the lesbian community. Surely this is at least partially due to the greater time commitment that lesbian sex generally entails (to be bored ten minutes is quite different from being bored for an hour!)—yet I am also sure it is not *entirely* physical, for certainly even gay men and heteros would eventually rebel against torturing themselves even a few minutes a night several times a week over the course of their lives.

No, the problem is mostly lesbian—or most *seriously* lesbian—and, although it will destroy suspense, let me give you the diagnosis right here: I think the problem with lesbian sex stems from the fact that, in lesbian sex, two women are involved—two women, in fact, who are *usually* (but not *always*) "lesbians."

●

What is a lesbian? A lesbian, supposedly, is a woman who has sex with a woman, or rather, a woman who wants to have sex with a woman, whether or not she's having it, or, rather, a woman who, if the choice were between a woman and a man, would, other things being equal, choose a woman. Some lesbians would choose women at all times and places; some might prefer a man—or some particular man—in certain circumstances; some would never have sex with a man at all, no matter what the circumstances. But this, in a way, is begging the question, for if a lesbian is a woman, what *is* a woman? Thinking about this, I realize I'm not only not sure what women *want*, but even what women *are*.

For instance, I'm a woman in a very different way from my mother; in many ways I'm more like my father than my mother. Does that make me a man? Does that make me a woman and my mother a male? Did that make my father a female? I'm different than some young 16 year old female model I recently read about in the Times; I'm even different than Martina Navratilova (though I really am rather similar, now that I think about it, to k.d. lang—I'm her older sister, perhaps, or maybe I *am* her—have you ever seen the two of us together? *Not!*) I could go on, but the point is, I am much more similar to many men, or perhaps dogs or cats or even chimpanzees, than I am, say, to Imelda Marcos or my mother. Let me put it this way: at least sometimes I feel I know what's in my cat's head, but I almost *never* feel I know what's in my mother's head. What we've got in common—what women have got in common—is our genitals, that's all—& in the case of transsexuals, not even that—or rather, if a man can be considered a "woman" because the inside of the penis is somehow turned into a vagina, then that makes becoming a "woman" just some kind of technological trick; looked at in that light there really is no difference between men and women except the brain, & in that sense no two brains are alike, so in a sense no two sexes are like, or at least, no two sexual preferences are alike.

But really, this is bullshit. I certainly *act* as if there are two sexes—I go to the ladies room, for instance, rather than a men's room—and I go to a gynecologist several times I year and I don't know a single man who does—so I certainly *function* as if there are certain differences between men and women, at least physical and medical differences, for in the more superficial areas—like clothing—you are just as likely to encounter me in the men's as the women's department. Even when I'm wearing men's clothing and cut my hair real short I'm still considered a "female"—you don't have to dress or wear your hair "like a female" to be considered female—no, it's a question merely of the genitals, or rather, the *shape* of the genitals—because doctors don't actually *change* the tissue of the sexual organs of a transsexual, they merely change the *arrangement* of the tissue: making what was external *internal* in the case of a male-to-female transsexual, and making what was internal *external* in the case of a female-to-male transsexual. (Notice how, in the universe, the female characteristics area *always* internal, whereas the male ones are always external!) So it's this *rearrangement* of *tissue* that's considered necessary for officially and legally changing one's gender—and this rearrangement is evidently crucial not just legally, but emotionally and psychologically, to the transsexual him/herself, for if it was enough to know what oneself was *regardless of shape,* no one would go through the time and expense and medical and psychological hazards of an actual sex change. At the very least, part of being a woman is *being perceived as a woman,* both by the world and oneself, which apparently has at least *something* to do with shape and hormones, although not necessarily dress or hair length. In one sense transsexualism can be seen as a failure of the imagination, an insistence on the conventions of womanhood being on literal and un-ironic display—though as a transgressive act it certainly makes for very strong theater and is in that sense *evocative*—rather than *demonstrative*—of imagination.

Is a transsexual a woman? Is, possibly, a transsexual more of a woman than I am?

Certainly transsexuals have definite opinions about penises—which is that men have them, and women don't— the final transsexual stage seeming to be either the acquiring of or disposal of the penis: which means that transsexuals are more unequivocal about the presence or absence protruding organs than are of most lesbians, who, although they don't have fleshly penises, almost always possess a sampling of latex simulacrae of various sizes, shapes, and colors. Perhaps male-to-female transsexuals use dildos too, and this would make an interesting study, the preference of the artificial to the real, which again points up the inherent theatricality— perhaps I should say *melodrama*—of the transsexual.

Anyway, although officially women *don't* have penises, most lesbians like to pretend at times they do; or rather, like to *pretend to pretend* they do, because of course there is no real pretense, but only the pretense at pretense.

●

If it is fairly obvious why intercourse with a dildo is pleasurable for the receptive partner (because the physical sensations from a dildo are not all that different from a penis, if more so from fingers), and less obvious but still apparent why it should be pleasurable for the *active* partner in dildo intercourse (due to the pyscho-sexual power of topping), it is even less so why the giving and receiving of blow jobs should be so—both to the person giving the blow job and the one receiving it. That there is pleasure there can be no doubt, or people wouldn't do it—at least they wouldn't do it more than *once*. I've participated in such acts, from both sides, though I prefer the sucking, and I think the person whose dildo I sucked—rather, the person who *wore* the dildo I sucked (for the dildo may, after all, have been mine) got pleasure out of it, because she got wet. As far as I know this is usually a sign of excitement, at least when somebody isn't peeing by mistake. This person wasn't peeing, although I have to admit this dildo-sucking wasn't, like some other sexual acts, the final destination, but rather a stop along the way.

What kind of stop? A mental stop, primarily, at least for the person having the dildo sucked, as of course there are no actual nerves in the latex. This is not to say she experienced no physical sensations, for no doubt the dildo bumped against her, which could cause certain sensations in or around the clitoris or vaginal areas, & for myself I could certainly feel and taste and even *smell* the latex in my mouth. But although these are physical sensations they're not what are normally called "sexual" sensations, or even "sensual" sensations, and I think no one will dispute that the pleasures of dildo-sucking and having a dildo one is wearing sucked are essentially conceptual in nature. Of course, now that I think of it, what pleasure I used to get when I took an actual flesh penis into my mouth was of a mental nature also (although, to be utterly frank, most of the time it wasn't any kind of pleasure at all!).

There is a perception that women smell and men don't, but I don't find this at all true. Nonetheless, at times, I must confess, I did get a certain kind of, say, *pride*, in having this power over someone else—which is a power, primarily, of being able to give or withhold pleasure. But this is not the same mental pleasure that I get from sucking a dildo—which is not pride at all but more its opposite—*degradation*—though really, sucking latex, viewed from the outside, is, if anything, *silly* rather than *degrading*—but I suppose the degradation comes from the idea of being forced to take this thing in one's mouth—though of course one is not "forced" at all (even though one may *pretend* to be)—but maybe it is the *desire* that is degrading, the desire to suck a latex cock as if it were a real cock, though of course we all know it's not real, and since it's not real, why should it be more degrading for me than for the person who's pretending to enjoy having it sucked? After all, in terms of physical sensation, I have more—in my mouth and throat, even the pressure on my knees if I'm kneeling, and this includes not just pressure but taste and smell—than the person being sucked. Actually, I guess what we're doing is *pretending* to be participating in a degrading situation, and I suppose there is a point-of-view from which, in fact, such a *pretense* might be considered degrading—if one defines a desire to be degraded as a "degrading desire." Anyway, this notion of submission and power is what animates those mild physical sensations and pressures and tastes with pleasure—though this pleasure could disappear in retrospect (as mental pleasures can) if I found out later (suppose I had been blindfolded) that my partner was, say, sleeping or reading a book while I sucked on her dildo, and was in fact entirely unaware of this putatively degrading transaction. In other words, part of what enables me to take pleasure in the dildo-sucking scene is my assumption that I am engaged in a *mutual* fantasy of degradation in which, albeit ironically, my partner and I both pretend to be excited, and by this shared pretense *do* manage to become—albeit in a half-hearted fashion—*actually* excited.

When I said that if my partner was reading a book or sleeping and wasn't aware I was doing or *had done* this sucking I would lose, in retrospect, my pleasure in the fact, is subject to one *caveat:* that is, there is the possibility I could transmute the pleasure of being engaged in a *mutually acknowledged degrading act* to one of being a being *so* degraded that I could enjoy a solitary degrading act both of whose subject and object were myself. But even this "meta-pleasure" is still subject to the fact that the Other must be made aware, in retrospect, of my pleasure in this solitary degradation, and *acknowledge* it as degrading: otherwise, I could theoretically be just as content sucking a dildo that is not attached to a person, a dildo that is not even being sucked in the presence of a person—but I am not. That is, I *imagine* I am not, for, to tell the truth, I must admit that my evaluation of my lack of pleasure in solitarily sucking a dildo is merely theoretical, as I have, in fact, never sucked a dildo by myself alone in a room. But as I tend to have a fairly good anticipation of what I'll enjoy, the fact that I have never desired to do this—not even *now* for the sake of this essay—makes confident in asserting that not only would I not get a lot of pleasure from it—but my lack of fantasy concerning this act is very *proof* that I would not enjoy doing it.

By the way, the fact that one can re-evaluate the pleasure of a sexual act makes clear, once again, and very specifically, the mental component of sex, and the way in which the meaning of the experience can be altered even in retrospect. Which is very far removed from the realm of pure sensation.

●

There is something in gayness that likes perversity, that is drawn to the excitement and danger of the forbidden. Up until recently, homosexuality *itself* was that *inherently transgressive act,* and the charge from violating the norms, and from the mutual recognition (usually in forbidden places) of others who were also violating those norms, maintained its force, even over time. During the early years of the Gay Liberation Movement, the erotics of the verbal confession of our preferences (in the ritual known as "coming out," which partook not a little of *epate-ing la bourgeoisie*) were used to replace the eroding erotics of secrecy, as did our appearances as acknowledged outlaws in such public venues such as marches and demonstrations.

But with the growing acceptance of homosexuality, with same-sex partner benefits and homosexuals in public office, with an (albeit apparently heterosexual) NBA star routinely appearing in make-up and dresses and a well-known transvestite granted her own tv show (it wasn't long ago that "straighter" segments of the gay community fought to keep transvestites from appearing in Gay Pride parades), it is increasingly hard to pretend that society is terribly outraged—or even interested—in what gays and others of our natural flamboyant 'kin' do in—or even out of—bed.

Even as we applaud, we mourn, for if the world needs "outlaws" against which to posit a norm, just as surely do "outlaws" need "norms" against which to posit "outlawness." Almost certainly it is this erosion of the conception of homosexuality as an inherently transgressive act that is destroying gay—but particularly lesbian—*eros,* and which forces us to greater and greater extremes of transgressiveness in order to evoke the same pleasurable outrage which we obtained so easily in the past.

Looked at in this light, perversity is not just a by-product of queerness, but the very essence of it.

Looked at in this light, it is clear why so much of gay art seems designed to tweak the noses of the Jesse Helmses of the world—*because who else really cares?*

Why does this *particularly* affect lesbian *eros*? Because it is not implausible to assert that whereas in some sense an imbalance of power is almost *inherent* in the activities between men and men, and women and men, this is certainly not the case with women—either in our bodies or the ideology of feminism—and that we therefore must subsitute role-playing and the various forms of pain and bondage and fetish object use to create a sense of opposition and dichotomy (and even repulsion) on which sexual erotics so strongly depend.

●

Consider what it *is* (as opposed to what it *means*) for a woman to top. Whereas both gay and straight males penetrate with their penises, which undeniably have sensation, women use their fingers, which have more sensation, obviously, than a dildo, but less than most other parts of the body—*not* because fingers have fewer nerve endings (they have *more,* even, than the sexual organs!), but conversely, because this organ is so overstimulated that in some sense we become numb to its effects. What I feel, really, when I put my finger inside a woman is, mostly, warmth and wet. It's odd, I like water a lot, I drink many glasses of it a day, I'm a swimmer and scuba diver, I fish, I like sailboats and kayaks, but the wetness inside a woman's body is different and sometimes, I have to say, I'm just not in the mood for all that gooiness, plus I start worrying about whether my finger is going to get wrinkled. (I'm ambivalent about sweat too, not on me but other people.) In addition to wetness my finger also feels skin and sometimes the cervix through skin and although that feels okay that's probably *not* what we mean when we say we "really enjoy touching someone." We mean it as a kind of psychological thing, making a woman excited and so on, or sometimes (especially if she doesn't want but we quote "make her" do it) as a way of showing our power, etc. I mean, at least, to the extent I get excited touching someone else, I tend to get more excited more by the *idea* of this and what this implies about power and her relationship to me, rather than merely the physical sensations of warmth and wetness and skin against finger. (This is obviously even more so in the case of penetrating with a dildo.) In the case of being with someone for the first time, when the question of whether you're exciting her and whether she likes you, this touching can be *very* exciting, acting as a kind of objective correlative (or, if you prefer, *sign*) of emotional connection. In the case of someone you've already decided you "love"—or *could* love—this could, in fact, be the single most exciting moment of the entire relationship.

What about going down on someone? Oddly, although I'm squeamish about gooiness on my fingers I don't mind the gooiness of oral sex, perhaps because the mouth, due to saliva, is an organ of inherent gooiness, and also because we're used to putting all kinds of strange wet stuff in our mouth. So sucking on a woman is similar to putting some strange food in our mouths—sushi often being used as a metaphor (by women) and fish (by men, well, really faggots who may not even have experienced women). Smell is important, so important that, in those rare cases when someone's smell repels us, we are unable to sustain a relationship, however much we might otherwise like the person. But even with such women I never think of spitting out goo, as years ago I wanted to do with men (but rarely had the nerve to insult them by so doing), although—oddly—I do not enjoy getting this goo secondhand—say, by having to suck it off my finger. Perhaps then, it's not the goo I don't like, but sucking my finger. To be absolutely honest, I even find it disturbing to both lick a woman and touch her at the same time, and I *particularly* dislike touching her after she's been licked and is really wet. I like to be consistent, I guess, by ending up with the same organ I started out with; whether this is due to a sense of esthetic minimalism, or some form of obsessive-compulsive orderliness, who can say?

Anyway, although going down on someone does entail a lot of physical sensations involving touch and taste and smell, I'm still pretty sure these are *not* what we define as sexual sensations. This is *not* because my mouth has no sexual sensation—I have at times in my life been sexually aroused by kissing somebody—but I don't get aroused in that particular fashion by oral sex. What sexual arousal I do feel—not always but on occasion—is in my genital area—which is odd, when you think about it—but I'd have to say that even here *most of the time most of the pleasure* is a kind of mediated pleasure, a *mental* pleasure—in the idea of giving pleasure to somebody, or perhaps rather the power of giving pleasure to somebody—which implies also the power of *withholding* pleasure, which I am in this case (and nearly always) choosing *not* to do, which makes me able (also) to congratulate myself for my kindness, which, in all honesty, I often think of as pity—pity for the partner who is so in my power and whom I could disappoint if I so chose—and I have a kind of empathy for her for being in this subservient position to me. Sometimes my recognition of this empathy gives me a kind of sexual flash through the genital area, but this is a kind of arousal of myself by myself, by the *idea* of myself as a good person. You'd think—when my partner is having an orgasm and I am not (& since I am much better with my tongue than my hand, my partners almost always come when I'm going down on them rather than touching them)—that instead of feeling sorry for them, I'd be *jealous* of them (especially as I don't always find it so easy to come), but this is not the case, at such moments I *don't* experience jealousy, though often I *do* feel irritation—on rare occasions *such* irritation that I very subtly try to prevent them from coming, by altering my movements in a way that would prevent *me* from coming (changing position, changing speed, intensity, etc.), but that, unfortunately, has no such effect on them.

Thus, although I say I "like to go down" on people, this is clearly a complicated kind of liking, in many senses no liking at all. It may mean "I'd rather go down on someone than stick a finger in them," or it can mean "I'd rather go down on someone than have her go down on me;" it can even mean, in these complicated times, "I'd rather go down on someone than have a fight—or even a discussion—about why I don't *want* to go down on them." Other times, I use the phrase "I like to go down on people" to mean that it's an act I do well and I take pleasure in doing something well, like the pride of a craftshuman in a job well done. (Here I'm forced to admit that although I still give a pretty good blow job, years ago I used to do it a whole lot better, and even now when I do it relatively well there's still a tinge of melancholy about the fact that I used to do it so much better in the past.) It's not exactly that I've forgotten how to do it, it's more that I've lost the desire to do it as well as I used to. I still have *the desire to desire* to do it well, but not the actual *desire*. Is this true for everybody? Is this part of the problem of sex, or just of getting older?

In any case, whether I get less pleasure in going down on women now because I don't do it as well, or whether I don't do it as well because I don't get the same pleasure from it as I used to, the great feeling of pride is gone. A *little* pride yes, and also kindness and consideration for my partner, and also (I'm sorry to say) *contempt*—for those times when I give an indifferent blow job and my partner still comes—which I take to mean she cannot discriminate between a good blow job and a bad blow job—or at least an *indifferent* blow job. (I *could* interpret this vainly, and assert that by comparison even my lousy blow jobs are, in the scheme of things, still relatively good—but I won't!). Which means, in effect, that I am wasting my efforts going down on someone who doesn't even have good taste. This lack of discrimination naturally makes me like them even less, which makes the whole exercise even *more* pointless—except on those occasions when the *aim* is for me to like someone less—if, for instance, I like someone so much more than they like me that I desire to even the score by shifting the power from them to me. On the other hand, my tastes don't run towards the taking of power, but rather towards surrendering it, so there's a bit of sadness in the regaining of my power—the same sadness, but to a lesser degree, that comes with falling out of love.

Oddly enough, though I've often regretted the fairly low quality of blow jobs I've received in my life (a former lover once said there was "no point" in learning to do it better since she'd never be as good as me!) I have never really wished that I could have experienced one of my own blow jobs.

Why not? Because "I" would be doing it, and there would be no surprise.

●

What is a good blow job—and why couldn't my former lover learn to do it better? Because she was hung up on *mechanics*, when the question is *empathy*—an imaginative reconstruction of what the other person is feeling inside oneself, so that, in the great heyday of my blow job giving, I'd know what to do not just in general but in the specific *next* second what *this* particular person wants at *this* particular time—and not just because of a pattern of breathing and sounds (which is merely using feedback), but because of some deeper connection or knowledge. That kind of connection takes a big effort, it cannot be faked, it's like Method Acting rather than a more external English style of acting—and the thing about acting a sad scene in method acting is that you actually *become* sad, even if it's for a different reason than that for which the character in the play or film becomes sad. So, years ago, because in some sense I had to *become* the other person to give a good blow job, I got *sexually* aroused by giving the blow job, which means in a sense I was giving it to myself after all.

Because such imaginative reconstructions are so difficult and tiring, perhaps it's not so surprising that most people don't give very good blow jobs; most people are insensitive and lazy, and no more empathetic to the people in their beds than they are to the needs of strangers in the streets. Varying one's rhythm here and there in arbitrary fashion the way most dykes do is really no different than giving a buck to someone without really looking at them: it's responding to a generic situation rather than a specific person. Even so, most lesbians still give a better blow job to women than most men, not because they "try harder," but because of some vestigial empathetic reflex that, however muted in "real life," resides in the body.

Anyway, mental pleasure is what, I suppose, "stone" butches want and choose, and also, at least to some degree, s/m tops, who don't always get touched or achieve orgasm. But what about the rest of us, who engage in what is called 'reciprocal sex,' what is our pleasure—the pleasure of *being touched*— about? Is it possible this is purely mental too?

●

I would not have written this essay, of course, did I not intend to assert that it was. I claim that even sex that appears to be purely physical is really largely mental in mental, hence in some sense imaginary, and it is this mental quality of it that eventually causes a lack of interest in one's partner—or perhaps even in sex in general. I'm not sure whether this is an inherent condition of lesbianism—in that a tendency towards a mediated response may predispose one to becoming gay (it may just predispose one towards fantasy)—or a response to the way the condition of lesbianism has been dealt with in our society, which may therefore be subject to change. But I'd also like to say that, if it's a response that is subject to change, that the nature of lesbianism—whatever that may be—will have to be redefined as well.

●

Of course, despite all this, people still have sex—even boring old, unmediated vanilla sex. Even I do it on occasion—despite the disappointment I *know* is *inherent* in the act (insofar as it falls so far short of the Ideal act, which can be purely imaginary or an actual moment in the past that has become crystallized in an ideal form). But the only way is to affirm, before the commencing of activities with one's partner (ironically, of course, as humor is essential to postmodern sex) the essential *pointlessness* of the activity and the likely dissatisfactions that may attend it—not just the inability to orgasm, but the possible absence of pleasurable sensations—because only in this articulation of future disappointment do we eliminate the *tyranny of expectation* which (in our perverse way of being) is the only way to create a space in which satisfaction *may* actually appear. Then, and only, then, should one dare to touch the other—in places, I would suggest, that have no name, no official function, whose location is merely proximate (e.g. "back of the knee," "the lower thigh"), and in a manner that does not automatically *assume* a progression towards the clitoris or vagina, or presume that *orgasm* is the natural culmination of any "sexual" (in its broadest sense) act. It is only in this freedom from the prescribed, the official, the named, from movements to which discourse has already staked its name—in the interstices between where we are *supposed* to get excited and where we *do* get excited, in the movements that are *supposed* to thrill us vs the movements that *may*, on occasion, *actually* thrill us—that pleasure may re-surface—not in the relatively unconscious or "innocent" manner of our youth, but partially, contingently, and with full knowledge of how it cannot be as it once was. . . .

There is more to say, of course, but, as the pleasures of anticipation and titillation are far greater than those of fulfillment and satiation, I will save them for another time and place.

Acknowledgments

"Strange Attractors" was published in the anthology **Bad Sex** ed. by John Hoyland, Serpent's Tail, England, 1993

"The Duchess of LA" and "Butch" are from the novel **Don Juan in the Village,** Pantheon Books, 1990. "Butch" also appeared in **High Risk: An Anthology of Forbidden Writings** ed. by Amy Scholder and Ira Silverberg, Plume, 1991

"The Kiss" is from the novel **In Thrall,** Clarkson N. Potter, 1982

"I Flunked Masturbation Class" was published in *Crawdaddy,* & was later anthologized in **Very Seventies: A Cultural History of the 1970s from the pages of Crawdaddy** ed. by Peter Knobler & Greg Mitchell, Simon & Schuster 1995

"An Eye for an Eye" is from **Some Do**, Macmillan, 1978

"Glimpses" was originally published in *The Paris Review*

"'Total Time' at the Kiev" is from **Real Estate,** Poseidon Press, 1988

"Faithfully Yours" was published in the anthology **Infidelity** ed. by Marsha Rowe, Chatto & Windus, England, 1993

"The Ontology of Post-Modern Sex" was written for a lecture at the Bra Bar in NYC given Valentine's Day, 1996; a greatly abridged version was published in *The Boston Phoenix, One in Ten* supplement in January 1997

Photo by Robert Giard

About The Author

Jane DeLynn is the author of the novels **Some Do, In Thrall, Real Estate,** and **Don Juan in the Village.** She spent two months in Saudi Arabia as a correspondent for *Mirabella* and *Rolling Stone* during the Gulf War, and has published articles, essays, and stories in magazines such as *The New York Times, The Daily News, The Boston Phoenix, Harper's Bazaar, Tikkun, Redbook, Paris Review, Burn, The Advocate, Exceso, Avenue, Elle Decor, 7 Days, The Observer, The Washington Review of the Arts,* and *Mademoiselle.* She has been included in the anthologies **High Risk: An Anthology of Forbidden Writings; Bad Sex; Infidelity; Tasting Life Twice; Particular Voices: Portraits of Gay and Lesbian Writers; The Best of Crawdaddy; Testimony: Contemporary Writers Make the Holocaust Personal,** and **First Love/Last Love: New Fiction from Christopher Street.** She has had plays produced at the Theater for the New City, Encompass Music Theater, Club Chandelier, and the EEGO Playwrights Gala; her play *"The Cowgirl and The Blonde"* received first prize from Calliope Theater Company in Williamstown, (although it was subsequently censored and never performed). She wrote the libretto for *The Monkey Opera/The Making of a Soliloqoy* (music by Roger Trefousse), which was produced at the Brooklyn Academy of Music in New York and later showcased at The Opera America Conference. She has taught at Lehman College and The Writer's Voice in New York City, and currently divides her time between her homes in New York City and Long Island.

This book was printed in April 1998 by BookCrafters, Chelsea, Michigan, for Painted Leaf Press. The text is set in 11.5 point Officina Serif and is printed on acid-free paper.